LOOKING FORWARD

AND OTHERS

Looking Forward
AND OTHERS

BY
BOOTH TARKINGTON

Essay Index Reprint Series

 BOOKS FOR LIBRARIES PRESS
FREEPORT, NEW YORK

STANDARD BOOK NUMBER:

8369-1384-1

LIBRARY OF CONGRESS CATALOG CARD NUMBER:

74-93381

PRINTED IN THE UNITED STATES OF AMERICA

CONTENTS

LOOKING FORWARD TO THE
GREAT ADVENTURE

LOOKING FORWARD TO THE GREAT ADVENTURE

A T THE dinner table, the other evening, one of the ladies announced her hearty approval of the new morals for young people. We had been wondering if it could be really true that the modern young people are as "wild" as we so often hear they are; and this lady, who has a daughter of marriageable age, said she thought they were. She thought they were even wilder than we had heard.

"What's more," she said, "I'm heartily in favour of it. In the old days, when we were young, the boys had all the fun. They went on larks and enjoyed themselves just exactly as they chose, and the poor girls not only had to refrain from larks themselves, but had to appear shocked if they heard about the jamborees the boys had been on. Nowadays, what's fair for one sex is considered fair for the other. Our own generation is greatly scandalized by all these stories it hears of 'wild girls', but what's the actual truth of the matter? Simply this: our old-fashioned

hypocrisy has been swept away and a lot of unfair-
ness with it. My daughter has just as much right to
a good time as her brother has. Of course, I hope
they'll both be rather moderate about it."

Apparently what this lady said was accepted by the
other members of the party as reasonable; but later
in the evening, as I sat by the library fire with my
old friend the Doctor, I asked him what he thought of
it. He is sixty-seven years old and has seen many
"modern views" come and go—views upon young
people and old people, views upon right and wrong,
and views upon life and death.   He had said nothing
when the lady set forth her opinion upon the modern
young people, and he began his reply to my question
by explaining why he hadn't spoken.

"It might have started an argument," he said;
"and of course arguments only confirm people in their
own opinions. Her statement reflects a view that is
rather fashionable just now. In substance it's this:
'Since the boys enjoy dissipation and the sensual
pleasures of life, why shouldn't the girls?' Well,
that's not new. It's only another way of saying,
'What's sauce for the gander is sauce for the goose';
and it's founded on a belief in the wisdom of a
much more ancient saying than that—one you'll find

pretty generally prevailing throughout history during periods of prosperity, and sometimes, too, during periods of pestilence."

"What saying is that?" I asked him.

"It's the most desperate of all the sayings that have come down to us," the Doctor answered. "It's the expression of civilized man's most ancient despair; yet we've just heard it from the lips of a Twentieth Century lady who is much in fashion. It's man's confession that his life seems to him but a moment of consciousness between two eternities of black nothing. 'Eat, drink, and be merry, for to-morrow you die!' Wasn't that what she *really* said?"

"Yes, I suppose so," I said. "Are we in the midst of a revival of that ancient desperation? Is it the 'modern spirit'?"

"I shouldn't go so far as to call it that," he answered; "and yet I believe there are more people seeking mere pleasure nowadays—every sort of mere pleasure—than at any previous time in the world's history."

"Yes," I agreed. "But at the same time I believe that more people are seeking light upon the great question than ever sought it before."

"What great question?"

"Well, it might be put in the terms of the ancient saying," I suggested. "'Why *shouldn't* we eat, drink, and be merry, since to-morrow we die?' In other words, multitudes of people ask for confirmation of the old religious faiths because they can no longer accept the faiths unless they find the confirmation. Science has slowly increased agnosticism, until now there is great bewilderment. The churches feel it, and seek to offer us the confirmation by altering the letter of the faith. That satisfies the objections of some people to the old letter of the faith, no doubt; yet the confirmation remains as lacking as before. The lady at the dinner table was typical of the many who have come to the conclusion that no confirmation is possible. 'There's nothing for all of us to do, except to go on whatever larks we can,' she virtually said. Well, what's the answer, Doctor? You're sixty-seven; you've seen a great deal and you've thought a great deal. Have you any confirmations to offer, yourself?"

He laughed musingly. "I have my own for myself," he said. "Yet it has always seemed to me that confirmations were pretty obviously to hand for people of open mind. The open mind is the first necessity, of course. 'There ain't no sech a animal' as a hippopotamus for the old woman who disbelieves in hippopotamuses, even if she's looking right *at* one of 'em! You asked, 'Why shouldn't we eat, drink, and be merry, since to-morrow we die?' Well, the easiest answer is another question: But suppose you *don't* die? And the confirmation the world is seeking is confirmation of the ancient but shaken faith in that supposition. Man wants to know if he has eternal life and if there is God. If he finds an affirmative answer to either question, he'll accept it as the answer to both. If he finds that death is merely a change in continuous life he'll believe there is God. Isn't it curious that in the beginning man knew perfectly well that death was only a change in life, and not extinction of himself at all?"

"In the beginning?" I asked. "You don't mean the Book of Genesis, do you, Doctor?"

"No," he said. "I mean man before he is civilized, man before he is even barbaric. I mean the savage. The savage doesn't think about it; he simply *knows* that he doesn't die when his body dies. It's only after man begins to try to think the whole thing out with his little mind that he begins to doubt. He tries to get a complete plan of the universe inside

a seven-and-a-quarter-size hat, and the misfit makes
him desperate. So he decides to eat, drink, and be
merry, because his misfit thinking is too much for
him. But about what savages know, I'd like to tell
you a story, if you don't mind."

"Go ahead," I said.

"A good many years ago, I had a friend who went
up the Congo with Henry M. Stanley," he said.
"After a while, my friend was left in charge of a
section of raw jungle with a few native villages in it
along the river. He was the one white man in several
hundred square miles, and he had to be diplomatic.
Of course, he couldn't interfere with any of the
native customs; and so, when the chief of the village
he was living in died, and preparations were made to
burn a number of the dead man's wives and slaves, as
part of the funeral ceremonies, my friend had no way
to prevent it. Naturally, he was badly upset over
such a horrible thing; but he was entirely powerless.
He told me that he wanted to go away, where he
couldn't see them making the pyres ready; but he
couldn't—an unpleasant fascination kept him hang-
ing about, looking on.

"Just before sunset, they brought the victims out
and lashed them down upon the piles of brushwood,

and still my friend couldn't break the spell and get away. There was one man he was particularly sorry about—the old chief's head slave—and the torch was applied to his pyre first. That started the white man for the jungle; but to save his life he couldn't keep from looking back as he went.

"The smoke was drifting from the pyres, and the little crackling flames were beginning to grow longer, rising upward. Then my friend saw a singular thing: the new chief, who was the dead chief's nephew, leaned down over the principal slave, and whispered in his ear. This was the last the white man saw of the fearful business; he went into the jungle, as far from the noises and the terrible smell of that smoke as he could get, and he spent the night there, pretty sick.

"Next day he came back to his hut in the village, and he told me the thing he couldn't get out of his mind was the new chief's whispering in the ear of the old chief's head slave after the flames had already begun to scorch the poor fellow. What on earth could the chief have wanted to say to a man who would be dead within five minutes? What *use* could there be in saying anything to a man who was virtually extinct already?

"Well, he told me the thing puzzled him so that he finally went to the new chief and asked him about it. He said, 'Would you mind telling me what it was you said to your dead uncle's head slave after they'd lighted the fire under him?'

"'It wasn't important,' the new chief answered. 'I just told him to tell my uncle that the war canoe he left me was rotten.'"

The Doctor concluded this little narrative with a wave of the hand that left it to me to make my own inferences; so I followed the suggestion of his gesture. "I see. The slave was going to meet the dead man within the next few minutes, so he was a proper message bearer. Or at least the savage who sent that message thought so."

"He didn't think it," the Doctor said. "He knew it. He knew it as well as any man can know anything. He knew it natively, so to speak, and without reasoning or arguing or thinking about it at all. Savages accept personal survival of death as a fact as simply obvious as the fact of life itself. Of course, that's why they send along some of the wives and slaves of a dead man to go with him, just as they bury his weapons with him, and put food and water near his grave for him. They don't evolve a theory of personal survival, they simply are conscious that they will themselves survive; and deep within us all that same consciousness is buried among our other buried consciousnesses that perhaps we inherit from our savage ancestors. Plato was aware of such a consciousness of his own, and his wasn't buried. He said he didn't know whether other people were immortal or not; but he knew he was, himself."

"But Plato wasn't an ordinary man," I suggested. "If the rest of us do possess this buried consciousness, as you say, I'm afraid we'd find it pretty hard to dig up. Besides, I've heard it explained as rising from the savage's seeing himself in dreams. He concludes he must be two persons: the one he sees in dreams, his soul; and himself, his body. At least, that was the explanation."

The Doctor shook his head. "No, it wasn't an explanation, because it doesn't explain; it was only an attempt to find another way round the bush. The other self, seen in dreams, is possibly the result of consciousness of an unbodily self that actually exists. But I admit that our buried knowledge of our own survival would be difficult for most of us to bring to the surface. What that old consciousness

amounts to now in our civilization is something the
skeptics and agnostics and materialists would likely
enough call a tradition. Men used to believe they
had souls—spiritual parts that survived death; but
this belief and all of their other beliefs have given
way wherever they have not been confirmed by
science and reason. So the agnostics would say,
wouldn't they?"

"Yes," I said. "That's what I've been saying,
myself. We're looking for confirmation."

"Then let's try the confirmation of reason," the
Doctor suggested. "Let's see if it fails us. Other
confirmations are possible, of course, and thousands
of excellent minds accept the 'psychic' one of the
'spiritualists.' They may be right, for all I know;
but, so far in this matter, we can only fall back on
our individual experiences; and mine hasn't been
convincing. I've seen and heard some inexplicable
things, and so have most people who have been at all
persistent in seeking light after this fashion of seeking
it; but I have had no proof that I ever communicated
with dead people—no proof that a careful lawyer
would accept, I mean. So, for the confirmation we
seek, I found long ago that I had to fall back on my
reason. I, too, am not Plato."

"Did you find the confirmation there, Doctor—in your reason?"

"Let's see if you'll think so," he said. "Let me ask first, if there seems to be anything about me that will not perish if my body perishes. Well, that's simple enough to answer, because we know that the life that is in my body now isn't going to perish, but will only pass into other forms. Leave my body upon the hillside and its life will make a richer blossoming there; none of the life is lost. As for the rest of me, we accept it as true that nothing of me that is matter can be annihilated.

"Now, if you are a materialist, you believe that all of me is force or matter; so, therefore, since force or matter cannot perish, but only changes, you must believe that all of me is imperishable. That is to say, you may disperse me, but you cannot annihilate me. When I die I only change into other forms. A little water from the ocean has become a raindrop for a moment, then returns into the bosom of the sea. It no longer has a separate existence, but you cannot deny that every bit of it still has existence. Everybody is willing to admit so much, I take it."

"Yes," I said. "Probably not many people will quarrel with you there, Doctor."

"Very well," he returned. "Then we must take a curious position. Since the material part of a man is imperishable, then, if he has a perishable part, it must be a part of him that is not matter. Therefore, if he has a spirit, and if any part of him perishes, that part must be the spirit. So you see where the materialist comes out. He must admit that his body is immortal, and that the life in it is immortal; but that his soul, if he have one, may be finite. I said just now that this was a curious position to be driven into, but it's more than curious. If you'll think of it for a minute or so, I think you'll agree with me that it's ridiculous."

"Wait a moment, Doctor," I said. "The materialist won't admit, of course, that he may have a soul—a spirit, that is to say, apart from matter."

"Good enough," said the Doctor. "If the materialist won't admit that he may have a soul apart from matter, then he must admit that he may have one that is not apart from matter; and if he admits this, he has admitted, according to his own definitions, that possibly he has an immortal soul. Altogether, I should think the logic of materialism about as unreasonable and unsatisfactory as the foggiest mysteries of mysticism. Of course, the literal fact is that the materialist believes he hasn't anything in the nature of what people think of as the soul, except his brain. He believes that when he dies, his brain and he, himself, simultaneously cease to exist, because his brain is himself. Have you ever seen a brain in a jar of alcohol?"

"Yes," I said. "Why?"

"Because," the Doctor answered, "if you have, and can believe that such a thing produced wireless and the Taj Mahal and Gray's 'Elegy,' I want to take another look at your eyes!"

"You want to take another look at them in order to see if my brain is affected, do you, Doctor?" I asked, and when he promptly replied, "Yes, I do," I thought he had fallen into my trap. "We don't think well, then, when our brains are affected, do we?" I said. "Gray couldn't have written the 'Elegy' if his brain had been damaged, could he?"

"No," the Doctor answered. "No more than Paganini could have made music with a broken violin. But Paganini with a broken violin in his hands would still have been a musician. The violin doesn't make the music, does it? Go a step farther back into Paganini, and ask how it was that he became a great violinist. Because his hands could do the necessary fingering? No; he had to train his fingers. That is, his fingers had to be controlled and made to do their work by his brain. 'There we have it!' says the materialist. 'It was his *brain* that did the real work!' No; that can't be, because he had to train his brain too. He had to make it learn a great many things, acquire a great many things, before he became a finished musician. *Who* had to make his brain do all this? Paganini did. Then there was a *person* behind his brain, was there?"

"There may have been," I said. "But a number of people would say that heredity did it, and that what made him train his brain, or a part of his brain, was merely a hereditary pressure of activity in another part of that same brain."

"Whose brain?"

"Paganini's," I answered.

"Then Paganini owned a brain, and an activity in one part of it trained another part of it in music?"

"No," I said. "Of course, if I admit that Paganini 'owned a brain' the materialist's case is lost, because I'd have to admit the existence of the owner—a person or identity behind the brain. The materialist's answer is that there was no such owner. There was no Paganini except the brain. One part of it had a hereditary impulse, and trained another part of it in music."

"Very well," the Doctor said. "What was the origin of that hereditary impulse?"

"Some remote ancestor of Paganini's evidently had a special turn for music."

"All right. Where'd he get his 'special turn'?"

"From a remoter ancestor."

"All right again," said the Doctor. "Let's go back to the first of Paganini's ancestors who had a gift for music. How did he get his talent?"

"It couldn't have been a talent originally. The first of Paganini's ancestors who inclined to music did so because of environment, or accident, perhaps. He may have come into possession of a fine reed pipe, or perhaps he lost a leg, and had to make his living playing on a harp."

"Let's suppose he lost a leg," said the Doctor. "And that he saw no way to make his living except by playing the harp, for which he had no talent. One part of his brain evidently had to say to another part, 'Here, you've got to learn to play the harp.' Well, what made the directing part of his brain *able* to say such a thing? It didn't have any hereditary musical activity, so how could it put forth such a command?"

"It was able to draw conclusions," I said. "It had the power of reason."

"Where did it get that?"

"Inherited it," I said.

"All right; that puts us back where we started. Paganini was musical because he inherited an activity in one part of his brain from a first musical ancestor, who was musical because of a hereditary activity in one part of *his* brain that made him able to draw conclusions. Let's go back to the first ancestor who could draw conclusions. Now, since this one couldn't have any such hereditary activity, where did his brain get that power?"

"I don't know," I said. "Nobody knows."

"Pure mystery, is it?" the Doctor inquired.

"It seems to be, so far," I admitted. "I could say, of course, that Paganini's first reasoning ancestor evolved the power to reason out of the pressure of environment, but that would only throw us back to the beginnings of evolution and the original life cell; and the mystery would confront us there just the same."

"Which is the same as saying that materialism is as much founded on mystery as any other theory.

That is, materialism is just as much mysticism as
mysticism is itself, isn't it?"

"Certainly."

"All right," the Doctor said. "Then the materialist is a person who has a choice of guesses. He
looks at a brain in a jar of alcohol, and he arbitrarily
decides to believe that there, actually before him,
minus the stimulant of blood circulation, is a real
self of St. Paul or Isaac Newton or Abraham Lincoln.
'*It* thinks,' he says; not, '*He* thinks.' Some of the
ancients believed that the kidneys were the seat of
the mind; others thought its seat was the liver; but
even they believed that the liver and kidneys were
only the *seat* of the mind—they didn't believe that
the liver and kidneys were the *people*. They never
confused Socrates or Alexander or Charlemagne
with viscera. Well, experimental science has discovered that the brain is more vitally the seat of
thinking than is any other part of the body. You
can change an ordinary man's way of thinking by
doing various things to any other part of his body,
of course; but the brain is the vital centre of the
whole nervous instrument, and that is all we know
about it. My brain is a part of my possessions, in

the sense that my liver is a part of my possessions; and I admit that, if either is damaged, I shall be in great difficulties to go about my work; but neither of them, nor any part of my body, is *myself*."

"And yet," I said, "if a part of your brain is altered a very little bit, your whole nature will be changed."

"My expression of my nature will be changed," he answered. "But I shall still be myself. Let's go back to our useful Paganini. Change the tensity of one string upon his fiddle, and his music will become discordant. Suppose you loosen all the strings and twist the violin, while he is compelled to go on playing until his instrument is irreparably damaged, just as I might be compelled to go on living in a damaged condition until my brain and body were finally wrecked. He would be the same Paganini, and the music he *wanted* to produce would be the same, though the sounds would be mad. And if you'd heard Paganini play under such conditions you'd have called him mad, though the angel of music that dwelt in him was an angel none the less. He was not his fiddle, and destroying his fiddle would not destroy Paganini. I am not my brain, and destroying my brain will not destroy me."

"I hope not," I said.   "But couldn't an agnostic charge you with reasoning too much by means of analogy?"

The Doctor laughed.   "I dare say; but I'd retort by defining an agnostic as a man who refuses to reason by any means at all.   He accepts only what he *knows;* and, as he knows nothing, his acceptance is naturally rather limited.   Well, let's admit that none of us *knows* anything worth knowing, neither the mystic, the agnostic, nor the materialist.   Man on this earth is like a boy being educated; he can get only what knowledge he is able to comprehend; but if you'll look at man historically, you'll see that he is granted the opportunity to learn as fast as he *can* comprehend.   His professors know algebra; but they can't explain algebra to him until he has mastered some arithmetic; as soon as he's *ready* for algebra they begin to explain it to him.   To my mind the most significant fact in man's development is that he does actually receive knowledge in exactly the same manner that a schoolboy receives it.   We sometimes speak of 'attaining to knowledge'; but to me knowledge appears to be received through the attainment of ability to comprehend it.   For instance, let's consider our knowledge of how to fly.

In my own young days, a person who believed flying possible for men was considered a foolish visionary. We'd just got accustomed to regarding railroads and the telegraph as about the topping achievements of the human mind, and it wasn't thought possible to go much farther.

"Of course everybody *wished* that men could fly, and yet, except a few cranks, everybody said that men could never fly. Some said we 'weren't intended to'; others said it was 'scientifically impossible'—inventors who worked on models of flying machines were thought crazy; and people who believed in the possibility of flying were derided. Indeed, a man who 'believed in flying' was about on the plane with the man who believed in ghosts. I don't think, though, that the experimenters in flying were considered nearly so respectable as the ghost hunters of psychic research are considered to-day. And yet all the while there existed the possibility that men would fly. Possibility? No; the *certainty*. That certainty was in existence, as it had always been in existence, waiting for man to discover it and use it. It was merely waiting for him to know enough to be *ready* for it.

"For thousands of years men had been longing to

fly, to know the freedom of the air; their longing had been a real one, a genuine great hope; and yet they laughed at themselves as fools for having it. It was the idlest of dreams; and dreams were for poets, not for practical people. Other great hopes had attained their fulfilment; but this one was too impractical—too mystic! So that when it actually came to fruition and the Wrights were in the air, day after day, many people were still incredulous.

"When the stupendous sight of men flying in the sky was offered to the farmers near Dayton why were most people still reluctant to believe that this great hope had been fulfilled, and that the dream of men for thousands of years had come true? It was certain to come true, for, as I said, we know now that it was a certainty. But why didn't we know *then* that it was?

"Well, there's an answer, and it fits in with our inability to know anything that we can't comprehend. In other words, we won't believe anything unless we know the 'how' of it, or unless somebody in whom we have confidence makes us believe that *he* knows the 'how' of it. As soon as we heard that the Wrights had fitted a little gas engine to a kind of box kite, we said, 'Oh, yes, I guess it must be true, because *that* way they *could* fly.' But ten minutes earlier we'd hardly believed a word of it.

"Yes, man is a schoolboy, going to school; and, like a schoolboy, he is pretty sure that he knows what he knows. For instance, he used to know that the earth was flat. Well, there came to be a great deal of pother about that, in the course of time. Accepted science ruled that the earth was flat, and everybody, except a few queer people and mystics, knew it was flat. The materialists won't accept any statement that can't be backed up by the five senses, or by mathematics, and the earth was flat to the five senses: you could *see* that it was flat. Were you going to believe a theorizing mystic who asked you to credit something directly opposed to the evidence of your very eyesight?

"Earlier in man's history he beheld the sun in the heavens, and every material evidence proved to him that the sun was his god. When the sun was kindly, man's crops bore plentifully. Man was happy in his god's friendly beaming. But when the god was angry and veiled his face in black, misfortune fell upon man. There in the sky was visibly the direct cause of his weal or woe. How could anybody deny that the sun must be the god of man and the earth? Mystics said, 'No. The sun is not more a conscious person than is any other fire. There *is* a god, true; but the sun is only the true god's instrument.' So the people burned those mystics for their impiety in insulting the visible god. Mystics have always been offensive to practical persons who can believe only in what they already believe, and already believe nothing not perceptible through the five senses. Isn't it queer, then, that ever since the world began, the practical-five-senses-materialist people have been wrong on every question relating to the nature of man, of matter, and of the universe?"

"Have they?" I asked. "I didn't know they'd been wrong *every* time."

"They have, though," the Doctor said genially. "Every single time. They believed that the sun was God, and kept on believing it until they couldn't burn all the mystics who believed otherwise. They believed that the sun was God; they believed that the earth was flat; they believed that it was impossible for men to fly; they believed that the liver was the seat of consciousness; and they believe now that Thomas Edison is a few pounds of tremulous meat that you can put into a glass jar. They believe that my brain is myself, and that I have no existence, or

hope of existence, except as my brain keeps physical
life in it. Well, since they have been wrong in their
beliefs upon all such matters during several thousand
years, I am not so eccentric as to think that they
could possibly be right—for the first and only time—
upon this question, the most important of all."

"Then who is right?" I asked. "And what is
right, Doctor?"

"Let's see what our question is, definitely," he
said. "Since the life in us lives on, and since nothing
is destroyed, the question must be this: Have I a
'spiritual essence,' an identity and consciousness that
is not my brain and body? If I have, then it would
survive the dispersal of the body and the movement
of the body's life into other forms. Now, in answer
to this question we have the brain worshippers on
one side, saying 'No'; the agnostics in the middle,
sturdily insisting upon their ignorance; and the mystics on the other side, answering 'Yes.'

"We have just spoken of those who say 'No.'
They have always said 'No,' and they have always
been wrong. Who are the mystics, those who say
'Yes'? They are the savages, the intuitive, recent
sprouts out of nature, carrying with them up from
nature the consciousness of perpetuity—the sense of

personal survival that made the new chief give the
scorching slave a message for the old chief who was
dead. Those who say 'Yes' are the spiritualists,
and that increasing number of scientists whose study
of psychic phenomena has convinced them of the fact
of personal survival. Those who say 'Yes' are the
prophets of all the great religions, with their priests
and followers who died in the faith or live in it now—
all those myriads of millions of people who have accepted any of the great religions or accept one now.
Those who say 'Yes' are those who, like Plato, know
that they do not consist of brain cells. Finally,
those who say 'Yes' are those who have perceived
order and system and direction in the universe.''

"You mean that since there *is* system—which no
thoughtful or educated person can well deny, if he
knows anything about the 'orderly processions of the
stars,' for instance—then the existence of the system
can have but one explanation?''

"Yes," said the Doctor. "Especially a system
that presents such features as the one we were talking about awhile ago. I mean the feature of the
system—of the great Plan—that grants man knowledge when he is fit to use it and makes himself ready
to comprehend it. Is that a *coincidence,* do you

think? No; not more a coincidence than the stars completing their stupefying orbits with regularity and precision. Well, where there is system and plan and design there cannot be chance, there must be the Designer. So we who have perceived the Design as the intentional work of the Designer—and I see no option to perceive anything else—we are sure that the hope of survival implanted in all these billions of the Designer's human creatures must be a part of the Design, and an intuition of a part of it. That hope would not have been so universal were there no meaning in it—not in a *Design*. The hope of flying was a small and sequestered hope compared to *this* hope, yet it was fulfilled—when the time came. So shall we all know that we survive when the time comes to know it. The Designer does not waste the hopes of man. He gave them to man to use. You see I don't agree with the lady on any point at all."

"What lady?" I asked, for I had forgotten.

"The lady at the dinner table," the Doctor said, as he rose to go. "I don't think 'Eat, drink, and be merry, for to-morrow you die' a safe motto. Suppose eating and drinking and being merry now might be harmful to you after you die! Very likely they are, if you overdo them."

"What motto would you suggest as a substitute?" I asked.

He had gone to the door, but he paused in thought; then he said, "There isn't any motto that can take the place of that old pagan bit of despair. It will last a while longer, and then it will go into the waste basket as a piece of incomprehensible and obsolete nonsense."

"When will that be, Doctor?"

"It might be next year or next century," he said. "The knowledge may come at any time, and all men quickly accept it as established. *I* don't know when it will be." He laughed then, as he went out. "You see, I didn't know when men were going to fly, either," he said. "Yet that was a certainty too."

And after he bade me good-night I heard him confirming this to himself as he departed from the outer door.

"Yes, we learned how to fly—when the *time* came."

As for me, I went back to the fireside, and presently found myself thinking of a skull I had seen once in Italy, the skull of a saint, I was told by the people who had charge of it. And now, remembering what the Doctor said of great men's brains in alcohol, I was doubtful that the skull had ever contained the saint himself. He was in Paradise, they told me; and, however that may be, I am constrained to believe that he must be somewhere. Since every part of him must necessarily still be in existence, so must he, himself, be equally alive and immortal. He, himself, was certainly the most important part of him; the other parts were subordinate and served no purpose except as temporary and changeable possessions of his. To believe the inferior parts invested with immortality and the most important part perishable seemed to me like believing that a man's trousers, and not the legs within them, possess the life and do the walking.

This is a view I cannot accept—that trousers do the walking—nor can I believe that the saint whose skull I saw is now principally sap in the eucalyptus tree growing beside his grave. Let people who *can* believe such things believe them. For my part, I am too great a skeptic.

NIPSKILLIONS

NIPSKILLIONS

NIPSKILLIONS" was the jolly old captain's bitter word. "A nipskillion," he said, "is a man who has had all the liquor he ever wants and, because he doesn't drink any more himself, won't let anybody else have any!" This definition, a weapon ready to the hands of the convivial, makes the nipskillionery of the present article seem deliberately odious; and the writer admits with timidity that he is indeed a nipskillion. Formerly he held nipskillions and all their works in great contempt; but that is the necessary previous condition of a nipskillion: no one can be a nipskillion who has not formerly hated nipskillions. However, the nipskillion has this defence: Should not the scorched child warn others against playing with fire?

The trouble is that those who are playing with fire do not wish to be warned against it, because they think the play is pleasant. "Besides," they say, "the fire will not burn you if you do not play with it indiscreetly or too roughly." That is true, and it is not true. Some people do play with fire and are never scorched, but more are scorched than go scatheless, and others are burned to death. In brief, the nipskillion wishes the convivial to profit by his experience, but the convivial wish to have the experience before they profit, or else are sure they can so manage matters that what disaster has happened to others will not overtake themselves. Oftentimes they are right, and disaster never befalls; the unpleasant fact, however, is that no man is warranted in believing that the disaster will not happen to him. All those to whom it has happened believed that it would never, and could never, happen to them. Finally, the nipskillion is a man who feels that he is miraculously lucky in having been merely scorched; he knows that the disaster *could* have happened to him. He knows that his dabbling in alcohol has been mortally dangerous. He knows that the disaster can happen to anybody—absolutely anybody.

A few, more than scorched, save themselves from disaster at the last moment, and become the more vehement sort of nipskillions—recruits for the disappearing band of "temperance orators"; but most of them are content to mumble their sentiments to a friend, or to some fellow nipskillion; and thus one did to me, counting upon a fair amount of sympathy, even after our dry lunch at the club, where often aforetime, we had been jollier together. Here is both the substance and the texture of what he said:

I hate it! I admit that, and so of course I can't be quite fair to alcohol, but why should a person be fair to the devil? Oh, yes, I know that's the regular old-fashioned "temperance talk," and the fact is that for a while, in the first stages of revulsion, I did come pretty near being one of these fellows that make speeches beginning, "Boys, I carry a Bible in my hip pocket now, but last year it was a whisky flask!" (I believe they usually add a pack of cards.) "And a pack of cards in my breast pocket!" Well, I didn't get quite so far in oratory, and I do try to look at the question with as much reasonableness as I can.

But take my case: I thought I was all right, and I was gone before I knew it. In fact, I was gone for a long while and didn't know it. Then a miracle pulled me out—an actual miracle: I'd like to tell you about that.

My drinking was all for comedy. That's what nine tenths of American best-class drinking is for—comedy. In our hearts most of us really assume life to be a tragedy. The ego is in opposition to the law;

it can't do what it wishes to do, and never even discovers what it really does want. When we achieve our ambitions we find they have amounted to nothing; and desire gratified is only dust in the mouth. Old Solomon knew what he was talking about: our life is vanity, and will be vanity until man discovers something really worth knowing.

We can do interesting mechanical things, such as talking round the world with or without wires, or making pictures of our insides, or weighing the moon, but we know nothing important. We have not yet taken the first step toward understanding death. When we do understand it we shall probably be on the way toward understanding life. But in the essentials we are still as wholly a mystery to ourselves as Adam was to himself. All human beings after childhood have the sense of tragedy in this mystery, though most of them may not often be conscious that they have it. We are born in the lethal chamber, the date of our death probably already settled by natural destiny; yet we find time to kill one another by war, by law, or by marriage sometimes. We are polyps, mostly water, and easily squashed.

I'm glad that I am a painter and not a writer of

fiction like you. You playwrights and story writers
paint your little compositions in words, you would
say, but the trickery of your art lies in the fact that,
instead of merely framing your picture, you make
what you call an "end" for it. Of course, some of
you do write what you call tragedies, sometimes;
and some of you do turn human beings inside out
to be better understood; but even the best of you
still write (a great part of the time) stories and plays
that end in lovers' meetings—marriages presumably
happy. As if the happiest marriage were not at best
a tragedy, even by your own rule of fiction! One
of every pair of lovers, husband or wife, is doomed
from the first to watch the other die, and then live
on alone—or marry again, and then die! You put a
"happy ending" to your stories for precisely the
same reason that the thinking kind of man drinks—
to *get away* from life, to make moments that are bear-
able. Of course, I know your excuse that marriage is
truly, sometimes, the "happy ending" of a part of
life—of the story of youth.

Probably life wouldn't seem tragic if we knew more
about it; but our darkness is all we know, and darkness is tragedy. I believe that every man who has
the power of thinking feels this darkness and knows

himself immersed in it. He may know this only vaguely, not putting it into words; still, he knows it well enough to want to get out of it; but the age of light is unthinkably distant, and he can't. Therefore there is a pressure on him at least to forget the darkness for a while. To this end, that there may be moments of forgetfulness, man, by the grace of God, discovered the Comic Muse. Man learned to laugh.

Comedy is, so far, the only alleviation of life, except work and what is called faith. I should call it the third best thing in life. We value it that high. Ladies love jesters better than they love the solemn knights; and the romancers are wrong. The dullest soul alive frequently says, "Thank God for my sense of humour!" thinking his facial smile a precious power. We adore our comedians, and the movies' great clown is paid in treasure like Sindbad's! We will pay anything for laughter.

Well, there is laughter in alcohol. There are morose drinkers; there are people who want the warming physical stimulant; there are others who drink to conquer timidity, whether for a burglary, a rendezvous, or a luncheon; there are unfortunates who drink to forget some personal wretchedness; there is "society drinking," too—drinking against boredom, or to be drugged to endure a long dinner, or to sparkle at one; and there are ruinous things called drunkards who drink out of the mere habit, which has become stronger than the original prompting; but incomparably the greater number of Americans who drink, nowadays, drink for comedy.

It is not for the taste of the liquors, of course. A grown person, no matter how much he might like candy, would not go to a candy shop and stand, or sit, with a group of acquaintances eating candy at intervals for an hour or more. And it is not as a stimulant for work that Americans characteristically drink; they drink at the end of the day. No; it is for *fun!*

And there is a kind of fun in it; that's the trouble. In the first place, the senses are a little numbed; the body is, for the time, more content, and almost anything may seem a joke; laughter is readier. Then, with the relaxation, with the dispersal of caution, and of watchful dignity, incongruous things are said and grotesque things are done. Men ordinarily dull through reserve or timidity dare to speak whatever comes into their minds; they project the nonsense of creatures at the same time half-witted and keen-witted; they are revealed as unexpected comedians, and since all mankind loves the comedian, they are found lovable. That is, fellowship is produced, and laughter becomes the heartier because it is congenially shared. Consequences become remote, nothing seems to exist except the sunny present moment and laughter.

That was my case. It was all for comedy—the Saturday nights, here at the club, left me things to chuckle over all through the week's work. Then I began to spend most of my evenings with a little set—friends of mine and their wives, and a girl or two—people who knew one another pretty well, and went about together almost continually. We all liked a romp, now and then, and would frolic almost precisely as children do; but of course, we weren't children, and couldn't have frolicked much except for a liberal allowance inside. In fact, we couldn't possibly have endured as much of one another as we did, without alcohol. Alcohol for laughter! In the "last analysis" that was the tie that kept us together. We couldn't have lasted a week as intimates, on water; we'd have stayed home o' nights, or perhaps have gone to the theatre separately.

I'd got to cocktailing regularly, after five in the

afternoon, to be in livelier form for the evening; and
sometimes by the end of the "evening" there was
rough sledding.   Well, that was a gay little set of
people, no harm in them—except to one another!
Only one of the men ever got actually drunk at our
parties, and his wife was always indignant with him
when it happened.   That was one of our standing
jokes; the funny things Adeline said to poor old Pete
in her anger.   He couldn't "hold" as much as the
rest of us—not so much as Adeline, for that matter.
She blamed him bitterly, yet I suppose she knew in
her heart that they ought to stay away from our
parties; but she couldn't do that.   She was drinking
for comedy, too.

The set held together for several years, and most
of us lived more for it than for anything else—and
alcohol was our tie, don't forget!   Of course none of
us would have believed such a thing if it had been
stated in words.   I wouldn't.   If you had said such a
thing to me, for instance, I'd have told you to go to
the devil, and you wouldn't have done any good.   I'd
have said that I lived for my work; that I was cover-
ing canvas with as good stuff as I'd ever done in my
life, and that after a long strain in the studio I did

well by myself to relax in the evening among amusing people. The truth is that a lot of the things I painted then ought to be burned.

There came to be times when I had to drink a lot before I "felt it," and there came to be more of them when I desired—and needed—a drink in the morning. That's a rotten bad sign, but *I* didn't see it so. I took it as part of the joke—after I'd got the drink. After a while, then, I began "going on the wagon" for a week, or three weeks, or "until Christmas"; once I "stayed on" for four months. That's another bad sign, though there are some men in the world, I suppose, who wheedle themselves along and save their health and their business in that way. Naturally, the really "moderate drinker" never has to "go on the wagon."

Whenever I was "on the wagon," the thought of the jolly time ahead was continually in mind; I felt virtuous and worthy of the reward of a great and jubilant fall from the tedious wagon. My imagination was largely liquor; I thought of it, consciously, much more than when I was "off the wagon." It was a time of nervousness, irritability and yearning. I haunted the drinking of others, watching them thirstily, and pouring into myself sarsaparilla and

ginger ale and pints of aërated waters in painful
imitation of the happy pouring of the free. Then, at
last, came the merry, merry day—a date always set
according to some mystic theory, heaven knows
what!—and I would "fall off."

But I quit "going on the wagon." I thought that
probably some day I would "climb on" again; but I
declined to fix the day; I let it remain misty. Then,
finally, I never thought of it. By that time I was
living about as much on alcohol as on food, and I had
no conception of life apart from alcohol. I had a cocktail, or a small glass of brandy, as soon as I got up in
the morning. I had a cocktail, or two, or three, before
luncheon; I had a whisky and soda—perhaps more
than one—during luncheon, and a cordial afterward.
In the afternoons I got to the club at an earlier and
earlier hour, usually I had time for two or three cock-
tails before the crowd turned up and the *real* cocktailing began. Then came the cocktail with dinner,
champagne, cognac, and after dinner the protraction
and intensification—by means of indefinite whisky
and soda—of the effect already produced. What was
the use of producing it so elaborately if one was to
let it fade?

That question still strikes me when I see "moderate" people drink themselves throughout a dinner, into a little hilarity, and then grow lumpy and sleepy. My crowd always followed the hilarity up before the reactive slump came, and I think we were at least logical. I realize that people do need wine at dinners that are only to be endured by a little drugging, and that on the whole it is better to make the drugging mild and let it die in the diners when their duty and the dinner are done; but it would appear more reasonable to abandon both the dinners and the drugging. Nature never intended such dinners.

Nature never intended man to go *out of his way* to put alcohol inside him. I've heard it maintained that a certain amount of alcohol has a food value. All right: we get that much in food. "Food value" talk and the other "value" talk about alcohol is defensive hypocrisy. I know, because I was that kind of hypocrite myself once. The truth is that all drinking of alcohol is against nature. The honest drinker admits it; he says, "Yes, I'm hurting myself more or less; but I'll take the hurt for the sake of the comedy I get out of it." Man doesn't know much of Nature's intentions, all he can get is a hint, now and then; but he can tell only too well what Nature does

not intend. She does not hint of her non-intentions
to man; she either kicks them into him, or kills him
outright for emphasis. All pain is Nature kicking
us, just as all evil is our deafness to her hints. Well,
I got my share of the kicking.

My painting had gone pretty well to the dogs.
Not that I didn't still work at it; I did work, but I
cared more about something else. My real primary
purpose, daily, was to get outside the amount of
alcohol I needed, to be "up to normal"—the state
of nervous excitement and recklessness that renewed
my power to laugh again. Work was secondary, and
when it was a question of either working or drinking,
work lost the debate.

One of the most curious things about my condition
at that time was my failing to realize where I'd
dropped to. You see, I often thought I was thinking
clearly, but I never was. A man who drinks as I did
keeps himself in a glamour; and he's so busy drinking
himself up out of his depressions and the rest of the
time saying and doing all manner of excited things—
he never gets a lucid interval. A man "on the
wagon" for a period doesn't become really lucid, he's
got the return to alcohol somewhere in the back of
his head all the time. I'd passed the "wagon" stage

long ago, but I didn't realize where I was. I didn't
even have any self-pity, though I sometimes felt a
little mystified about myself. I was anxious to marry
a woman to whom, I'd been "respectfully devoted"
for a long time, and when, I asked her she seemed
startled and compassionate, and rather shocked—as
if a lunatic had proposed to her! Of course that did
give me something of a jolt; I almost saw myself
clearly that day.

I went through the customary physical humili-
ations: eyes bad, hands bad, heart bad, head awful,
until I got "up to normal" for a few hours, and then
everything worse next day. I couldn't think con-
nectedly, couldn't concentrate; I had no plans.
Really, I hadn't anything except alcohol. It was the
principal thing in my life. I was living for it. I was
gone!

Then the miracle happened. I quit. Quit com-
pletely. Forever. All in a minute—just like that!

I didn't plan to do it. I didn't even attempt to
do it. I just did it—or something did it for me. I
woke up one morning, after an unusually fierce night,
and when I crawled out of my bedroom for some
brandy I found I couldn't lift a glass to my lips.
That didn't alarm me, I'd been that shaky often, but

I decided to go back to bed and sleep until my nerves were somewhat quieted. I did go back to bed, and I decided to stay there until I got "up to normal" without alcohol. I stayed there all that day and the next—when I began to care a little about real food—and the next, and the next. I stayed there ten days, and when I got up I was feeble enough in body, but I'd given my mind or soul, or "something," enough rest for it to get a quiet and true vision of what had been happening to me, of what I'd *slid* into, so to speak. And I was through. I had decided. I knew I couldn't "drink moderately." I didn't want to "drink moderately." I wanted to drink immoderately—enough for comedy, a hearty laugh, not a mere little smile of quiet exhilaration. (The little smile kind of drinking isn't good enough for anybody except epicures, or true sensualists, or cautious and careful and cold-blooded people.) So I made up my mind, not that I would quit but that I *had* quit. There's an enormous difference! If you make up your mind you *will* quit, you face a struggle, it's my belief that you *create* a struggle. But if you say, "It's over—I've *had* my last," and say it with conviction, *knowing* it, and are quiet and resting when you say it, I believe that's all there is to it, and there won't be any struggle. There I was with the actual habit of years fastened on me; you'd have expected me to be in a kind of agony, summoning my will power and fighting, "wrestling with temptation," battling against the craving, the terrible thirst. Nothing of the kind. I had said to myself that I was through, and I had actually meant it. That was part of the miracle, and the rest of it was that there was no struggle at all.

There was no craving, no temptation, no thirst. It's true I did have all the liquor thrown out of my apartment, when I first got up; but I needn't have done it. I'd as soon have forged a check as touched it. I didn't *want* to touch it. All I wanted was to get back to a real world and away from the sham one that alcohol builds.

So I went to work in the studio, and gradually the old delight in work came back to me, the old capacity to see and do; and it took the place of the false comedy and excitement. Things straightened out for me. And after a month I came back to the club. I sat with the crowd, picked up a cocktail and sniffed it. I knew myself so safe that I wanted to see if I'd feel any craving. "Craving?" No more than I'd have had for so much kerosene!"

That's the point of my case: there isn't any struggle if you quit as I did. They tell me there are dipsomaniacs, and there may be some abnormal people who can't turn the trick; but I almost doubt it. And I don't believe there's the slightest question of will power. Never for one second did I consciously exert my will; there wasn't anything real to exert it against. I didn't say to myself, "I will," or "I won't." I said, "I've had my last," and knew that it was true. It didn't take the will power, or the strength, of a caterpillar. It didn't take *any*. I just rested a little and got my head clear.

After all, a miracle is only Nature doing something we've learned to expect her not to do; and my miracle is one that will happen to any other man who'll rest a while and consult himself. My recommendation is two weeks in bed with nobody about except some one to bring beef tea and toast. Simple enough, isn't it?

Yes, men drink to get away from life, to forget life by living for a time in comedy. But true comedy isn't in alcohol, after all. Alcohol is only the quick way to false comedy. The price is too high and the false comedy not worth having. But I suppose the others can't really *see* that—not until they get to be nipskillions, like you and me!

THE HOPEFUL PESSIMIST

THE HOPEFUL PESSIMIST

I

THOMAS J. GALLUP, of Gallup's Food Stuffs, Inc., had been so busy ever since he got out of college and bought an interest in a hominy mill that he'd never had time to think about anything except his business. "It's an actual fact," he told his physician, ten days after the operation. "I've been in a hurry for twenty-five years."

"That was one thing the matter with you," Doctor Parsloe observed genially. "Twenty-five years is too long for a man to be in a hurry."

"I begin to see so," the patient agreed, glancing ruefully about the big, blank-walled hospital room. "And I've just begun to wonder how it happened. As soon as I took on that first hominy mill—I bought it on a shoe-string and I never knew when the shoe-string might break—I got in a hurry. I *had* to be in a hurry all day and every day to make that mill pay for itself; and then, before it *was* paid for I saw a chance to get another and I took it on; and I went on hustling and enlarging the business, keeping in a kind of whirl, you know, and going to sleep late every night planning what I'd do next day, and getting up early to do it, and so on, month after month—and then the other day you came down to my office and jumped on me and sent me up here to get some new equipment in me, and you said that had to be done in a hurry, too. So those surgeons grabbed me and hurried me through the operation—and, well, sir, all of a sudden here it was 1924 and I'd been in a hurry since 1899!"

He paused and chuckled feebly. "Well, sir, I believe I've been doing more thinking, these last three days, since I got over the worst of the soreness, than I did in all the twenty-five years before. You see, it's the first chance I've had to stop and take a real think since 'Ninety-nine."

Doctor Parsloe, seated beside the bed, looked at him quizzically. "What have you been thinking about?"

"I suppose you might call it wondering more than thinking," Gallup explained. "Wondering what the dickens it was all about."

"You don't mean your operation, do you, Gallup?"

"No," Gallup answered. "I mean the hurry.

Long ago I'd made all the money I need; and as for carrying on the business, well, you say I can't go back to it for a year, and I know my absence won't do it a cent's worth of damage. Yet there I was, hurrying just as fast as ever up to the very minute you stopped me. Where was I hurrying *to?* Was it merely out of habit, do you suppose?"

"Well, that's partly the reason, no doubt," the physician returned. "But hadn't you set yourself some goal to attain, some point ahead at which you intended to stop and take a look around? Possibly you hadn't reached it."

Gallup laughed feebly. "But I had—a dozen times! At first I said, 'If I ever get a fixed income of ten thousand dollars a year, I'll quit. I'll take time to read and do some real travelling and some real thinking. But when I got that income I never thought of stopping; I was too wrapped up in my work. I said to myself, 'Wait till we've got a corporation that'll make our competitors sit up and take a little earnest notice of us!' And when that happened I said, 'No time to stop *now;* we've got to be the biggest in the field,' and when that happened, too, I said, 'Wait till we've forced our old rivals into the new combination,' and so it went; and so it would

have gone on till I dropped if you hadn't stopped me.
Well, what was it all about? Of course, I can please
my vanity a little by thinking that I built up a
'big business' and a lot of people get good dividends,
good salaries, and good wages on that account; but
I'm as selfish as the next man, and I wouldn't intentionally go on working myself to death to make
a lot of other people more and more prosperous. So
far as my intentions went, I was in it for myself, and
that's what makes me wonder why I didn't stop when
I reached any of those goals I set for myself. When
I was looking upward at the first one it seemed to be
the summit of a hill. I planned that when I'd
climbed 'way up there I'd build my house and settle
down in it and enjoy the rest of my life in peace. But
when I did get up there it wasn't the top; and now,
as I look back, I see there never was any hill with
a nice flat top for a house at all. My life looks to me
more like climbing a ladder that kept reaching out
of sight, and what I thought was top was only the
first rung. The ladder kept on reaching up and up,
and there wasn't any end to the rungs. Lying
here, wondering, it's begun to seem to me it isn't only
my own life that's like climbing a ladder: anybody's
life is climbing a ladder—a ladder in a thick fog.

You keep climbing and climbing, always thinking that some rung above you is going to be the top. When you get up there, you say, you'll stop and enjoy yourself. But when you do get there, you find it's only a part of your climbing, just as much as the rung below, and so you keep on until, *bang !* you fall off, some day, still in the act of climbing, and maybe you land in the cemetery, or maybe just in a nice cool hospital, with a pleasant nurse like Miss Cropsey there, and a philosophic friend for a doctor. But you never reach the rung where you thought you'd be happy. Now, what in the world makes you keep climbing toward that illusion?"

"Because the illusion persists," said the Doctor; "you keep on believing there's a top rung where you'll be happy."

"'Where you'll be happy,'" the patient repeated, and he laughed. "Yes; I guess that's what's behind everything else in every life when you get right down to it. Nobody ever does anything except try to be happy. Well, if that's true and everybody is trying to be happy, it means that nobody actually *is* happy. If you're trying to get to a place, you certainly aren't there. So it seems that everybody in the world is trying to get to a place called **Happi-**

ness and yet nobody ever does get there.   It's funny, isn't it?"

"But I know plenty of happy people," the Doctor objected.   "For instance, I went to a wedding this morning.   It was obvious that the bride and groom were divinely happy."

"Oh, no, they weren't," Gallup returned.   "They were in a condition of bliss, which is the state of forgetting, temporarily, that you aren't happy.   They were in much the same condition of bliss for a few days when they got engaged; then they went ahead and began planning the wedding, because of course they thought they couldn't be happy unless they got married.   When they've been on their hotel honeymoon a week or so they'll be planning to come back and build a house.   They'll decide they won't be really happy until they're settled down in their own little home.   Then they'll be worried at times until the baby is safely born.   How happy they'll be when that's over and they can be a grand little family of three!   And when the baby's born, pretty soon they'll begin to think how happy they'll be when they've got him through his teething and he begins to talk, and when they can get a perfect nurse for him—and when they can build a little larger house—

and so it goes on until they die. They'll often be
cheerful, they'll often be gay; sometimes they'll be
blissful; but their happiness will always seem to de-
pend on something ahead of them, and they'll work
for it, and when they get what they've been working
for, they'll have their little hour of enjoyment over it,
and then discover that happiness is still waiting for
them—at a turn in the trail ahead."

He sighed, lightly, as if abandoning the problem as
one not to be solved; but his physician was inclined
to be quizzically argumentative. "You said nobody
does anything except with the object of being happy,
Gallup. Take people who do bad things, for instance.
The papers are full of a man who murdered his wife
and then shot himself. He left a note declaring
himself an atheist. Was he seeking happiness?"

"Of course. He thought he was at least putting
an end to his misery, poor soul! That is, he believed
that what he did was the only step toward happiness
he was able to take."

"But people often do things that they positively
know will bring them unhappiness. I knew a woman
who deliberately gave up the husband she adored because she felt he'd be happier with another woman.
She condemned herself to a life of loneliness and

perpetual suffering. Was that seeking her own happiness?"

"Certainly," Gallup said. "She saw she was going to suffer either way; and she was so unselfish, she knew she'd be less unhappy if she made the sacrifice."

"How about a man who eats something he likes but which he knows will make him sick later on? Is he seeking this fugitive happiness ahead?"

"Yes; he mistakes a moment of pleasure for happiness, but the pleasure is still ahead of him when he makes the decision," the patient insisted. "You might have put a harder case: a prisoner under the third degree confessing to a crime when he knows his confession will hang him. Well, he's only found his present condition of misery so unbearable that the prospect of being hanged is less unhappy by comparison. No; I'm right. Nobody ever does anything except as a step toward happiness."

Doctor Parsloe laughed indulgently and offered a fresh suggestion. "You've been too busy to know much about what's called the 'new psychology,' I see, Gallup."

"Never heard of it. What is it?"

"Well, it's rather too elaborate for me to explain

in the course of a professional call: but its practition-
ers believe they've got more at the root of things
than you have. They don't agree among themselves
on all points, but in the main they seem to say that a
'survival instinct' is behind everything, and that
most of our actions and thoughts are caused by our
having sex. One prevalent view is that since the
lowest kinds of bugs have only the power to eat and
produce offspring, and as we've evoluted from them,
our principal motives must derive from sex and
hunger."

Gallup was already able to shake his head with
some vigour, and he did so now, in controversial
disapproval. "They're plumb off," he said. "Would
they trace Washington's farewell to his officers back
to a sex motive, for instance?"

"Yes, likely enough, or to a survival instinct, perhaps."

"I'd like to hear 'em do it," Gallup said. "But
suppose this 'new psychology' might be right about
our not having any fundamental motives that a bug
hasn't, and admit that all a bug at the bottom of
bugdom has got is his wanting to eat—because the
very bottom bugs haven't any sex at all; they just
bud their offspring, like a person's getting his wisdom

teeth and then shedding 'em, and probably the bugs don't *like* this budding any more than we do getting our wisdom teeth, though I watched 'em doing it in a biology course I took in college, and they did seem kind of indifferent—well, what I'm trying to get at is this: Suppose all the bug cares about is eating, *why* is eating all he cares about?"

"He must eat to survive, and all he has is his survival instinct."

"Think so?" Gallup inquired skeptically. "He goes floating around in the water, and he hasn't any eyes, of course, yet you might say he's looking for food, because that's certainly the only business that interests him. Well, he hasn't got any nerves, either, so you might say he can't feel to any great extent. You say he's got instinct, though, and you'd tell me that instinct is a kind of unconscious memory you have of your ancestors' experiences. Well, take the very first one of these bottom type bugs that ever existed. He must have done just what his great-great-great-grandchildren do, or he couldn't have kept *on* existing; but as he didn't have any ancestors, he didn't have any instinct. **But** he had *something*, didn't he?"

"I'm not sure," the Doctor responded. "It becomes a little confusing when we go back to the very first bug."

"You've got to, though," said Gallup. "When you're going back to origins, you can't stop halfway. You have to go back to the first or you haven't gone to an origin at all. Well, this first bottom bug couldn't have had any instinct; that's clear. And yet he went around looking for food. Something that preceded instinct made him do it. So what was that something? He couldn't feel and he couldn't think and yet he *knew* he'd be darned uncomfortable if he didn't find something to eat. Of course, he was mistaken, because he wasn't capable of any sensations; and yet he had the impulse and followed it. Well, that's exactly what I've been doing these twenty-five years. That first bottom type bug was following the same impulse that made me say to myself, 'I'll be uncomfortable until I get up that next summit, but when I'm there I'll be happy.' The bug was mistaken and I was mistaken, but the same thing made us hustle."

Parsloe found an objection to this. "It seems to me you're twisting things a little, Gallup. What animated the first bug was his impulse to survive. That's what made him uncomfortable if he didn't eat."

"No, sir! The impulse to avoid discomfort—the same thing as the impulse to seek happiness—was all he had. He didn't eat to live; he ate to be happy. What you call his 'impulse to survive' was his search for happiness. He was taking the first step, and by and by one of his descendants got a yearning and said to himself, 'I believe I'd really enjoy life if I crawled out on the bank among those reeds and took a snooze in the nice warm sunshine. He was our ancestor, probably, and none of us can escape the same sort of yearning; it's no use trying. The only man who can know that approach to happiness we call 'cheerfulness' is the man who thinks he is approaching happiness by working like a horse to get to it."

"But I know several perfectly happy men who don't work at all."

"Who are they?" Gallup asked.

"Well, one is a tramp."

"A tramp? You might as well talk about the Wandering Jew, or a 'man of leisure' shooting lions in Africa. A tramp moves on for ever seeking his happiness. He can't be even cheerful unless you

let him keep wandering. And of course you'll be
telling me you know people of 'happy dispositions,'
people who are happy no matter what misfortunes
happen to 'em; and people who are happy in their
religion. No; they may be serene or even ecstatic in
faith, and they may be cheerful by nature, or by
philosophy, as we say, but they all expect to be
happier some time ahead, and they all keep seeking
that time—*working* for it, unless sickness or old age
disqualifies 'em from working. And that's what
beats me!"

"What does?"

"Why do we do it? Since nobody ever attained
happiness, why do we keep on believing in it and
everlastingly working for it? We're like the donkey
with the wire fastened to his back and running forward to hold a wisp of hay dangling just beyond his
reach—he'd trot on till he dropped, always thinking
he was just going to get that hay. What makes us
like the donkey?"

"You might call it a universal urge," Parsloe suggested.

"Oh, you can *call* it anything you like," the patient
returned seriously. "I want to know what it *is !*
That's what I've been thinking about."

"Without reaching a conclusion?"

"Well, anyhow, I've reached a guess at it," Gallup said. "And a guess at the answer to a question of these dimensions is what we usually call an opinion. If you want to know what I think about your 'universal urge'—the impulse that makes us want happiness and work for it—I can't account for it without believing it must have been put into the first bug. He was the first, and he couldn't have created it, or acquired it by his own efforts; yet he *had* it, so it must have been given to him. Then it got into the rest of us—by inheritance, if you like to think so. But, when you look at what it's produced and compare Edison and the Woolworth Building with the first bug groping around in water, you can't help seeing that there's been a superior Thought behind such a business. I mean Direction. The urge must have been put into the bug intentionally, because there must have been a plan, and you can't have a plan that wasn't planned. That means there must have been a Planner."

Doctor Parsloe laughed, as he rose and took up his hat. "This isn't a death-bed conversion, is it, old man? You needn't worry. You'll be well enough to go back to your old harness—and the wisp of hay fastened before your nose—if you'll take a rest for a year or so. Do you think the pain you were having to stand last week was part of the Plan?"

"Naturally. The 'urge to happiness' is the force behind the Plan, and the 'urge' made me overwork without exercise or a proper interest in my insides; and then urged me harder *not* to overwork in that manner. The overwork and neglect brought me pain, which is a pretty hard nudge. Any plan has to have rules, or it can't be carried out. I must have broken one of the rules, you see, so I got pain, and pain is a *sharp* 'urge to happiness'—it points the immediate direction we've got to take. Then, if we think about it afterward, we ought to learn a little more about the Plan."

"You seem to have learned a whole lot about it in a few days!" the Doctor laughed, as he went to the door.

"No; I've only begun to see that twenty-five years is too long a time to be in a hurry," Gallup said cheerfully. "The 'urge to happiness' wasn't planted in us just to make us hustle. It wants to show us *how* to hustle—and it will if we'll take advantage of its hints. I'll think some more about it, before you come in to-morrow."

II

Outside the door of the hospital room, Doctor Parsloe met the comely nurse, Miss Cropsey, just emerging. She bore a tray that made it plain how well the patient had done by a light breakfast; and the physician, noting this without remark, asked how the night had passed.

"Pretty well," Miss Cropsey answered. "He wants to talk a good deal, though, whenever he wakes up. It's rather hard to get him to stop talking, once he gets started. I mean tactfully, of course—it's hard to stop him tactfully."

"It won't hurt him to talk—especially about something aside from his business. His operation is the first thing in twenty-five years that's taken his mind off his business," said the Doctor. "Let him talk all he wants to."

"Yes, sir," she returned, as she moved away. "The chart's on the dressing table."

But when Parsloe went into the room he didn't need the chart to tell him that his patient had continued to improve in the proper and expected manner. Gallup's greeting was hearty, in a voice with-

out tremor; and there was a reassuring vigour in his
grasp of the Doctor's hand.

"Sit down," he said. "You sit down and stay
awhile and listen to me. How long before you're
going to let me have a cigar?"

"We might begin to discuss that in a week or so,"
Parsloe returned, seating himself beside the bed.
"I suppose you won't be happy until you get it?"

"I won't be happy then," Gallup said. "I only
think I will. Didn't I tell you yesterday that we're
always believing that our happiness depends on our
getting something or other, but when we get it we
find happiness is still ahead of us, and never attain
it?"

"Yes; I seem to recall your expressing some such
pessimistic view."

"It isn't pessimistic," the patient objected
promptly. "I said there were times when we could
be gay or even blissful—and of course, it's our mere
duty to our fellow beings to be cheerful—but we
never achieve happiness. Yet what keeps us working
is our belief that we're on the way to happiness.
Happiness is a mirage always before our eyes; but
we don't necessarily move through a desert as we

struggle toward it—there may be many pleasant way stations, and parts of the road are often easy to travel. It isn't pessimism to see life like that, is it?"

"I incline to think so," the physician replied. "You see the 'urge to happiness' as the motive power of mankind, so to speak; and yet there *is* no happiness, you say. We're engaged in an unending race to nowhere. Nature plays a trick on us; makes us long for the rainbow's end, which doesn't exist."

"No," said Gallup. "The 'urge to happiness' is nature's plan of progress. We don't *reach* happiness, because nature doesn't intend that we should stop work. We find ourselves struggling on in the confusion of this strange world where happiness is impossible, yet hope of happiness keeps us everlastingly struggling on and on. The old-time preachers, when I was a boy, used to promise us happiness after death—if we never broke any of the Ten Commandments. 'Be good on earth or you won't go to heaven when you die,' they told us. 'Heaven' was just their word for 'happiness'; and they recognized the fact that it isn't obtainable on this earth."

"And you don't call that pessimism!" the Doctor laughed. "Why did you speak of our world as 'strange'? It's the only world we're familiar with."

"Yes, we're familiar with it," Gallup said. "A worm's familiar with the tree he's boring into, but he doesn't even know that it *is* a tree. The worm is contented, sometimes, till a woodpecker gets him; and so are some of us contented for a little while, sometimes; but of course, we can't have happiness in the midst of unknown surroundings. Ignorance may be a kind of fool bliss, but it can never be happiness, and we live in a great ignorance."

"We know a few things, though," Parsloe suggested.

"Precious few—we're wise only in comparison with the worm," said Gallup. "Certainly, we don't know anything really important about this world we're so familiar with. If you take the material view of life, we seem to live in a savage's universe, run by a kind of haphazard black magic. People are snatched from your side as you work together; the old friend who was so gay as he walked down town with you in the morning fell out of his desk chair at noon and was gone before his body touched the floor. Last Christmas you went in to look at the tree at your next-door neighbour's, and you talked about the pleasure it gave you to see his 'large and happy family rejoicing.' Well, they rejoiced; but can you say they were happy? No; they rejoiced because they made themselves ignore for a little while what was certain to befall them sooner or later. And that very night the young bride in the family went too near the candles of their tree, and a little flame touched her pretty dress as she stood there laughing. You couldn't do anything to keep her alive; and by morning she was only a pitiful memory for the rest of them. But if she hadn't gone like that she'd have gone another way in a little while. One by one, the others of that 'happy' family will be taken away, until there is only one left, and he will have had to bear all the partings, and then himself pass alone into mystery. And you called them 'happy'! No; the 'happier' the family, the more pathetic the tragedies before them appear to me. Life is pretty thin ice, I tell you. In our youth we go sliding over the surface, laughing; we see it give way under people in the distance; we hear them cry out faintly and disappear; but that can't *really* happen to *us*, we think; and we sing as we go. Then, after a while the ice gets thinner, and most of our comrades who began sliding with us have fallen through—some of them startlingly near us. Well, we still slide on, while the ice gets thinner and thinner under us, and we realize it *can't*

support us much longer—and the only singing and
laughter we hear is from far behind us, where the
young people haven't found out how thin the ice is
and how obscure the dark water underneath. No,
Parsloe; I shouldn't speak of happiness as part of
our sliding over that deep water."

The Doctor laughed. "I'm to understand that
this is optimism, am I? Might we call it the optimism of a gloomy convalescent?"

"Call it the optimism of a man whose convales-
cence has given him his first opportunity to think
about anything important since he started in business. But optimism it certainly is."

"My hearing must be peculiar," Parsloe said,
affecting puzzlement. "If what you've been saying
is cheering and hopeful——"

"You've only heard part of it," the patient interrupted. "If you'll be quiet a few minutes I'll show
you the optimism in it."

"By all means! I'm quiet already. Go ahead."

"This is how the thing appears to me," Gallup
said, staring thoughtfully before him at the blank
wall of the hospital room. "Sometimes we say we
come out of 'nowhere' into this world; but that only
means we don't know where we come from. We *may*

have come out of *some*where and we may go somewhere when we die—we can't properly say we come
out of nowhere and go nowhere. We come out of the
unknown and presently we pass on into the unknown.
Well, in the interval between these two unknown conditions we are in the condition we call 'life.' And in
this condition—while we're what we call 'alive'—
we find ourselves inescapably occupied in trying
to be happy. That is, we are always in action of
some kind or other, trying to get to be happier than
we are. We haven't got any power to choose
whether or not we'll be in such action or not. The
mind of any man never stops working, even in the
most sluggish forms of insanity; and there's no sleep
without dreams. You waken anybody from his
deepest sleep and ask him what he was dreaming;
you'll always find he *was* dreaming. So our life is
all action, either mental or physical, or both; and this
lifelong action is our search for happiness; and we
have no choice in the matter. Well, what's to be
done about it? Of course, this question means:
Can we do anything about it? Have we any choice
about anything? It's in the answer to this question
that I claim to be an optimist about our life.
In fact, I think it rests in any man's answer

to that question whether he's an optimist or a pessimist."

"I used to hear that a fellow's answer to your question determined whether he was a Methodist or a Presbyterian," the Doctor observed cheerfully. "You might explain further for my enlightenment, perhaps."

"I'm not going into theologies," Gallup said. "The theologies are going into themselves, nowadays, editing and even reversing their old forms, and a plain man can't tell much about 'em till they get settled down again—though of course he can agree with 'em on the main facts *they* all agree on. But what I was saying: it seems to me a man is a pessimist about life if he sees himself as without the power of choice between good and evil, which is to say he believes he has no choice between wisdom and folly or in any matter whatever. He believes himself a mere Jumping Jack—an automaton produced by evolution—or, in other words, our old friends heredity and environment. All he possesses, he thinks, is the consciousness of his own acts. He knows what he does, he admits, but *he* doesn't do it! *He's* just a Monkey on a String. Isn't it preposterous!"

"I'm not so sure it's preposterous," Parsloe objected. "I think there are some rather logical arguments for that point of view."

"Of course there are," the patient agreed promptly "There are logical arguments for almost any point of view. I remember a logical argument I made to my grandmother when I was sixteen. I absolutely proved my case to her by irresistible logic; and yet she was stubborn. 'Look here, Grandma,' I said— 'do you deny that what I've been saying is logical?' 'No,' she said. 'It's perfectly logical, but as it happens to be perfectly unreasonable, also, you're wasting my time!' I've always been on my guard against logic since then, and whenever logic wasn't reasonable, I've been sure it wasted my time. But I'll admit that *some* people in this world are mere Jumping Jacks, if you like. I'll even admit that most of us are only automatons at certain times. In fact, I'll admit that all of us are Monkeys on the String unless we detach the string ourselves."

"I don't follow you, Gallup."

"I was speaking a little vaguely, I guess," Gallup said. "I suppose the actions of most children are no more than hereditary responses to the conditions that surround them. For instance, give a seven-year-old descendant of selfish people a bag of candy, and he won't pass it around among his playmates; he'll try to sneak off alone with it—a purely Monkey-on-the-String movement of his; he can't help doing it. Well, we know that a great many grown people aren't much more than somewhat experienced children. A lot of grown-up and 'educated' people remain all their lives in the condition of beings merely responding to their surrounding conditions in a hereditary manner; they're automatons. For instance, I think I've been one myself, most of my life. I think I was a Monkey on the String up to the day you came into my office and sent me up here to the hospital. But since I've been here, I've concluded that I don't *have* to be one."

"How's that?"

"It's like this," said Gallup. "All those years that I was building up my business, I was going on automatically obeying the 'urge to happiness.' I sacrificed everything else to it;—you've shown me pretty plainly that I sacrificed my health to it, for instance. Also, I sacrificed what might have been very pleasant, a domestic life. Here I am at forty-four, an old bachelor with servants instead of children! Until now I've been just a hurrying slave of an 'urge.' True, I was responding to the impulse of progress; but I didn't understand the 'urge,' or myself, or what I was really doing. Now, I've been thinking for the first time, and I've concluded that a man can be superior to his natural responses;—that he can emancipate himself from what we're nowadays so fond of calling his 'reactions.'"

But here the Doctor's indulgent smile became more amused at the same time that it became more skeptical. "How can a man do that?" he asked.

"By using his mind to get some understanding of himself," Gallup answered. "And then by using his understanding to direct his will. Long ago I read somewhere that the truly wise man is one who can look down with serenity upon the mastered demons in his own soul."

"Would you call the 'urge to happiness' a demon, Gallup?"

"It might be one, so far as an individual is concerned, yes—if let to run wild in a wild mind," Gallup said thoughtfully. "It's rather likely to be a demon in young minds, sometimes—particularly in wild young minds. In naturally noble minds it can be an angel, of course. But what I'm talking about is the

possibility of our using it advantageously. It's a
universal force and we oughtn't to rest content with
being merely haltered to it and jerked along helter-
skelter by it, with sometimes our heads in the dirt
and our heels in the air. After thousands of years
we began to notice that something might be done
about electricity, you know. We weren't content to
let it go on doing nothing but tear down and burn
up houses and trees. Well, the 'urge to happiness'
is a much more important force, to us, than electricity
is; but I don't mean that Mr. Marconi should be
trying to box it up and send it by parcel post to
customers. I mean that every individual ought to
seek to learn more about it, though. I mean that
every man should study what the 'urge' does to
himself and how he can direct its effect upon him, because when he *can* direct its effect upon him, he has
the choice between what we call 'good' and what we
call 'evil,' or between wisdom and folly. He can't
choose until he can look down upon himself from the
heights of understanding, and observe his own
'reactions' and refuse to be bound by the demons
among them. He can't have choice so long as he's
only a slave to the old 'urge,' of course. That's
what I was for years, but now I've had my chance to

stop and think; and I've decided that henceforth I'm going to belong to the upper classes."

"What are you talking about now?" Parsloe inquired, frowning. "You're not going to found a new aristocracy, are you?"

"It already exists," said Gallup. "It has existed for several thousands of years probably. I know how fond we all are of classifying our fellowmen and that the classification is usually only a flattering definition of the classifier. The French noble used to see only two kinds of people: 'Us' and the mob. To the Catholics of the Sixteenth Century there were in the world only Catholics and heretics. To the modern bureaucrats of Russia there are only labourers, and 'bourgeoisie.' To Mahometans there exist only themselves and the eternally damned, consisting of all the rest of us. Well, I've got as much right as anybody else to make my own classification and put myself in the top class; and so, lying here and thinking it over, I've concluded that I see but two kinds of people in the world, an upper class and a lower class. The lower class tremendously outnumbers the upper, and in it there are all kinds of people except one. There are 'good' and 'bad' people in it, Catholics, Protestants, Mahometans, millionaires, Bolsheviki, kings, commoners, saints and thieves and politicians. The upper class is the small aristocracy of the world. I've just decided to join it."

"Then admittance is optional, is it?" Parsloe laughed. "Anybody who'd like to belong to your aristocracy can join if he wants to?"

"Yes, certainly," Gallup answered. "Admittance is optional. The lower class consists of all the great masses who blindly obey the 'urge to happiness.' Their movement is forward, but the progress of the slaves is tumultuous and anguished. The great whip, lashing across the universe, has the mob on the march, but the marchers trample onward, jostling and howling. The upper class consists of men who have said to themselves: 'Let us consider this whip. Let us consider our relation to it. Some of us fled into a by-path yesterday, thinking the whip meant to drive us there; and presently the lash fell upon us sharper than ever. Those who fled on by that way went into a more and more furious lashing until they fell and perished. Some of us took the hint and got out of that by-path. We infer that the whip means to direct us; and that when we are wise enough to understand its intentions we shall no longer feel the

lash.   In the meanwhile, having studied the hints of
the whip in the matter of certain by-paths, we need
not be slaves rushing blindly under the goad, but may
march with some dignity as thoughtful men studying
the direction intended by the Director.   To be more
definite, take the case of a jealous man.   'My only
escape from this torture is to avenge myself upon
the faithless one,' he says.   That is, vengeance will
bring him nearer happiness.   Then he walks in and
smothers Desdemona—and finds himself so much
further from happiness that he destroys himself,
perishing under the redoubled blows of the whip in a
blind alley.   But suppose this poor Othello had been
one of my aristocracy.   He would have considered
himself and his fury thoughtfully.   He would have
said to himself: 'I observe a passion of jealousy burn-
ing within me.   It would drive me to do murder if
I let it.   But I have observed that murder is never
a successful step toward happiness, but is rather a
movement in the opposite direction.   Moreover, all
the minor actions prompted by jealousy bring only
greater pain.   I have my choice.   I can act upon
the urgent promptings of my jealousy, which are very
sharply insisting that I obey them, or I can choose
to do that which my observation tells me would

in the long run be the course intended by the urge to happiness.' Having said this to himself, an Othello of my upper class would decide neither to do murder nor to act in any manner upon the promptings of jealousy."

"I see your point," said the Doctor. "But I don't see that Othello has any choice in the matter, since you imply that, if he sees both good and evil before him, he's sure to choose the good."

"No; the choice is always there," the patient returned. "I have a friend who eats pie at midnight, though he absolutely knows it will make him sick in the morning. What I said was that an Othello who belonged to my aristocracy would have looked down upon his jealousy and would have chosen not to be governed by it. In fact, an Othello of my aristocracy would never have married Desdemona at all. He would have said to himself: 'I observe that I am passionately in love with this lady, but the difference in colour will be disastrous eventually. I will return to Morocco.' The upper class of people consists of those whose understanding gives them the choice between good and evil and who choose the good. The lower class is all the rest of the people. That's my optimism, Doctor. I believe that there is an option in life for those who take thought to perceive it. They can choose which class to join."

"And you've decided to belong henceforth to the elect," the Doctor said as he rose to go. "That's good. How do you propose to set about it?"

"I'm not sure," Gallup replied. "I did evolve one rule of conduct, though. I didn't evolve it in my thinking since the operation. It 'came to me,' as we say, on the drive out to the hospital after you told me what had to be done to me."

"What was it that came to you?"

"I made up my mind," Gallup said slowly;—"I made up my mind that if I ever got well again I'd start in every morning and live the day through exactly as if I knew I had to die that night."

The Doctor laughed. "You were more apprehensive than you looked, I see! But would following that rule admit you to your aristocracy?"

"I'm not quite sure," said the convalescent. "I'll think it over before you come in to-morrow. I'll try to tell you then."

III

Doctor Parsloe found his amiable patient sitting picturesquely beside an open window. Almost touching the window, the upper foliage of a maple tree, just come into leaf, trembled and sparkled in the sunshine; but the bright window and bright tree were mere background, for Mr. Gallup himself was surprisingly decorative this morning, the physician observed. His grayish hair, grown longer during his illness than is the fashion, was becomingly smoothed, and, in his dark silk dressing gown, richly flowered, and with a neat stock about his throat, he had much the flavour of an early Nineteenth Century portrait of a thin but cheerful gentleman.

Doctor Parsloe's greeting went first to the nurse, who had just completed the composition of this portrait—in fact, she was returning a pair of silver hair brushes to the dressing table.

"You're making quite a swell of your patient, Miss Cropsey," the Doctor said. "You've got him up to look more like an elderly John Keats than an American tired business man."

She laughed; but she also blushed a little, as Parsloe was somewhat puzzled to observe. "I don't see the 'elderly' part of it so much," she said, and, with a friendly side glance at her patient, which he returned with a look of devoutest gratitude, she withdrew lightly from the room.

"Don't let her flatter you," Parsloe said; but, seeing that Mr. Gallup was smiling at the door just closed by the nurse, he inquired: "Have I your attention?"

"What?" Gallup asked; then replied hastily: "Yes, of course. Certainly you have my attention."

"I was about to offer a comment on what appears to be a contradiction," the Doctor said, looking at him rather sharply. "Yesterday and the day before, when I was here, you insisted that no such condition as happiness could exist for any human being. But this morning your expression would indicate that you might safely be called a happy man."

"I am," Gallup returned promptly, and at once corrected himself. "I mean I think I am. For the moment I've forgotten how unhappy I really am, and so I'm under the delusion that I'm happy."

"That's interesting. Perhaps you've discovered the way to join your aristocracy. Is that what makes you happy."

"My aristocracy?" the patient inquired vaguely. "I don't——"

"Yesterday you said there were only two classes of people in the world. One class consisted of most of us ordinary people; the other was the aristocracy;

you defined an aristocrat as a person who looks down
from the height of understanding upon all his own
impulses, desires, 'reactions,' and so forth, and then,
regardless of their urgings, chooses to shape his conduct to conform with the direction his observation
has shown him that Nature—or what you called the
'urge to happiness'—intends him to take. You said
that you were going to join the aristocracy, and that
you'd think it over and tell me how you meant to set
about doing it. I suppose you've discovered the
method and that's what makes you think you're
happy this morning."

"Yes, I remember," Gallup said. "It isn't what
makes me think I'm happy; but I did think it over.
In fact, I talked about it with Miss Cropsey for an
hour or so; and I believe her suggestions gave me
considerable light. I've concluded that the way to
become a member of the true aristocracy is to think
of yourself as if you were some other person."

"And would you think of other persons as if they
were yourself?"

"If you want to understand them, yes, that would
help," Gallup said. "But to get an understanding
of yourself seems to me the first step toward joining
the higher class of mankind. I must look at myself

as if l were a man interesting to me merely as a specimen, so to speak.   I must see myself as a specimen
whose 'urges' and 'reactions' should be considered
from an impersonal standpoint.   For instance, last
year I was clamouring for the income tax to be re-
duced on incomes the size of my own.   The taxes on
higher incomes than mine appeared to me as much
less unjustly injurious; and in that, you see, I was
like the mob.   A man of the mob feels that he's as
worthy as any other man.   He doesn't think this
over and try to find out if it's actually true; he just
feels it, and acts upon what he feels.   Well, if I feel
that I'm as deserving as anybody else, I have
naturally a feeling that it's wrong for anybody else
to have much more property than I have.   Anybody
who has more seems to have got it unfairly—to have
taken advantage of me in some way.   So I join in the
cry, 'Tax those scoundrels!'   But if I have become
one of the true aristocracy, I resist that impulse.   I
say to myself, 'My friend, it may or may not be
proper that the taxes should fall heavily upon incomes larger than your own—it is a question to be
solved by the science of economics—but what makes
you so noisy on the subject is mere vulgar selfishness.
You are shouting loudly about 'principles of govern-

ment,' whereas, what you really mean is that you want to keep your money and have other people pay the taxes. The fellow with less than you is trying to stick you to pay *his:* and so it goes on down the line of the whole mob. The truth is not in you until you cease to be of the mob."

The Doctor laughed. "So you were just one of the mob up to the day I sent you out here for your operation, were you, Gallup?"

"I'm afraid so. I was just a blind booster of my own business. Of course, I don't mean I was going altogether wrong, Parsloe. Not at all. I wasn't sitting on the fence, looking at my neighbour's big wood pile and saying, 'Some people have all the luck!' At least I was 'producing,' helping to build, and entitled to a little pride on that account. After all, work that builds something is the only satisfactory occupation in life."

"Are you sure?" the Doctor asked. "What about work that builds something ugly?"

"Ugly to whom?" Gallup returned. "You probably mean that some of our 'growing cities' would be ugly to a Sixteenth Century Florentine. They aren't ugly to the men who are building them, they're beautiful. After a while, when the men who tear down to build up have done their work and are gone, the cities will be beautiful even to an 'art critic'; but if a man of the building generation could come back to life then and look at a finished and beautiful city, he'd lament—he'd call it a dead town. The kind of beauty *you* like doesn't come, you see, until the kind of beauty *he* likes is dead. I'm not ashamed of having been one of the boosters and builders."

"But now you're stepping out, as I understand you," the Doctor said. "You're going to be one of the few emancipated people—the world aristocracy—who refuse to act upon their own motives."

"Yes, I am," said Gallup. "But I may be just as much of a booster and builder as ever, when you let me get back to it. Whatever I do, though, I'll do deliberately, without the old blind rush; and I'll take time to look about me, time to think, and also time for a little enjoyment. Perhaps my enjoyment may take the form of philanthropy—or golf—or both. I'm sure if life is an infinite ladder, we ought to make platforms on it, here and there, where we can get our breath and rest a little. We're beginning to learn how to do that. For instance, in my father's youth I don't suppose there was a Country Club in the United States. Men belonged to the militia or the volunteer fire departments, and sometimes they went hunting or fishing, but there wasn't so much recreation as there is to-day. It was considered the proper thing to be up early on Monday morning and work pretty steadily until six o'clock Saturday evening, winter and summer, until you were too old to work at all. Nowadays, we don't hold so strongly to that view. It began to break up with the coming of Country Clubs in my own youth; nowadays the great public parks are everybody's Country Club, and yachting had become the poor man's favourite sport. I mean land yachting—touring by automobile. Only a few years ago that was a distinguished amusement of the rich; but if there's an I. W. W. who doesn't indulge in it now, he must refrain out of prejudice. On the whole, Parsloe, our world is a pleasanter place to live in than it used to be, and I've decided to take some part in its pleasures instead of being the hurried slave I was until you stopped me."

"And that decision is what makes you think you're so happy this morning, is it?"

"No," Gallup answered, looking out of the window at the maple tree's tremulous foliage twinkling in the sunshine. Then he turned to the Doctor and smiled with a guilty hardihood. "I—I've decided—that is, we—we're going to be married, Parsloe."

He seemed to expect surprise, if not shock, to follow his announcement; but the surprise was all his own, for Parsloe remained inscrutably placid. "Yes," he said. "Naturally I supposed so."

"You did!" the convalescent exclaimed. "What on earth made you——"

"My dear man, I've had a little experience of most things during thirty years of practice. You're forty-four and a bachelor. For the last fifteen years you've been living at a club. Not since you were a boy at home have you known what it means to have a woman in charge of you. Of course, I saw what the result must be."

"But you don't even know who I'm going to——"

"I don't?" the Doctor interrupted. "It's Miss Cropsey, naturally. I knew it a week ago."

"You couldn't possibly," Gallup protested. "It wasn't settled until this very morning. I asked her not half an hour before you came in. So how could you——"

"It didn't need a prophet, Gallup! In our boyhood our mothers look after our clothes, our eating,
our health, our comfort, and our behaviour—that is
to say, our morals. Well, we 'go out into the world,'
free of our mothers' supervision, but deep within ourselves we remember it and crave it. We know it was
good for us, no matter how much we enjoy being on
the loose. Now, for years you've believed yourself
a fine example of a 'cynical bachelor.' You've
laughed at men who had to ask their wives' per-
mission to come down town in the evening. You
laughed because you saw married life from an out-
sider's viewpoint only. Wives in general have
appeared to you as bosses and husbands as the
bossed. You've rejoiced that you were not a cap-
tive, you've jeered at the captivity of husbands; and
yet, all the while, though you didn't know it, you
had within you the longing to be bossed yourself—
to be bossed the way your mother used to boss you.
She wouldn't let you go out and play with bad boys
in the evening, and she made you stay home when
you had a sore throat, you remember. Well, when
you found yourself helpless in a hospital and a woman
in charge of you—why, Gallup, of *course* it was bound
to happen! When a nurse is tactful and good-

looking as well as capable and the patient is an un-involved bachelor, the thing is almost as automatic as it is with a widower. I think I'd say it's been the more automatic in your case, because you're what's called a 'confirmed old bachelor.' Men of that type usually propose when their hair is being brushed by the nurse, or immediately after. You see, Gallup, you've been acting like a 'well-oiled machine.' You haven't had any choice, even in the matter of your own marriage; you've been an automaton—what you called a 'mere Monkey on the String,' the other day. But it's good for you."

Gallup looked thoughtful. "Well, perhaps that's true," he admitted. "At all events, it's very pleasant. And I sha'n't be an automaton in my married life. Certainly I can choose what sort of husband I'm going to be."

"That's interesting," the Doctor laughed. "What sort of husband will you choose to be?"

"I'm going to be an ideal husband," Gallup returned with simple gravity. "I can do it because I feel that I've got old enough to marry."

"You believe people under forty-four aren't old enough to marry?"

"Not intelligently," Gallup answered. "I incline to think that if people under forty or fifty marry successfully they have a lot of luck. I know the majority of 'em do come through all right in the long run, but it's usually after a good many anguishes that threaten smash-ups. The ideal husband and wife wouldn't have to pass through such painful adjustments—they'd begin right and stay right—and only middle-aged people have enough experience to know how to do that."

"How do they do it?" the Doctor inquired, surreptitiously much amused. "What is an ideal husband, Gallup? What are the requirements? What's the most important one?"

"I suppose you'll say I'm taking a 'very material view of life' and of women," Gallup answered—"but my belief is that the first and most important requirement in a husband is the ability and industry to support his wife and their children."

"Yes; I'd agree with you there," said Parsloe. "I'd say it's practical to assume that much as fundamental. The ideal husband must keep his wife and children in a reasonable measure of comfort according to their reasonable needs: and of course he should provide for their future. The good husband husbands the resources of the family. What's the next requirement?"

"I believe it's amiability—amiability expressed in courtesy," Gallup said thoughtfully. "He should be polite to his wife. The head man of one of my machine shops used to be my chauffeur, and once his wife came to see me about something. She seemed a mighty bright, lively little woman, and I asked her if she was always that way. She said she believed she was, and I asked her how she managed it. Well, she thought a minute; then she said, 'It's due to my husband, I guess. We've been married fifteen years and he's always just as polite to me as if I was a perfect stranger!' Now, that strikes me as pretty important, Parsloe. As a requisite for an ideal husband, I believe I'd put it before what we call the moral qualities, though of course he'd have to have them, too. He'd have to give his wife the pleasure of respecting him. He'd even have to give her the chance to be proud of him. Naturally, it's mighty valuable to a woman to see that her husband's respected by other people, but she can get along without that if she can be proud of him herself."

Parsloe laughed again. "I'm afraid you're asking

for rather Sunday-school-book virtues in your 'ideal husband,' Gallup."

"I'd ask more than those," the patient returned. "I'd ask him to be a domestic diplomat—to know when not to bring a friend home to dinner, for example. But, more than this, I'd ask him to try to continue to be interesting to his wife. I mean an interesting companion. He ought to find something that brings them upon congenial ground outside of their household and business routine. Golf, bridge, gossip, and the rest of it have their uses, but I'd call a mild excitement over politics or the French Revolution rather better—or music, or paintings, or beetles and microscopes. The 'ideal husband' ought to help to keep his mind alive—which would help to keep his wife's mind alive, too, of course. They ought to have something not personal to themselves to really *talk* about, I mean."

"That would be rather rare, I'm afraid," the Doctor said. "Husbands and wives talk plentifully when they're alone, I suppose; but the great care we take to keep them apart at dinners, for instance, is our recognition of the fact that as a rule they have no impersonal entertainment to offer one another."

"I don't think it's generally the fault of the wives," Gallup suggested.

"It's hard to say," the Doctor laughed, more and more amused by his friend's earnestness. "What's the next requisite for your perfect husband?"

"He ought to study his wife. He ought to find out secretly the things she does, or is, that she'd like him to appreciate, and then he ought to show his appreciation. He oughtn't always to do the expected thing. He ought to give her little surprises—I mean surprises of the kind he's certain she likes. Others might be dangerous. I mean, he ought to put some extra Christmases and birthdays into her life from time to time. He ought even to be a little extravagant about giving her feminine things—though by this I don't mean he ought to surprise her with expensive hats of his own selection. But if, now and then, he discovers that she's secretly longing for something she thinks too expensive—or involving too much selfishness on her part—and if he dashingly buys it for her and surprises her with it, well, I think he's helping to build himself up as a good husband. At least, I'm pretty sure his wife would think him one."

"His wife," Parsloe repeated thoughtfully. "We

haven't said much about the wife's part, we've been talking so much about what the perfect husband will have to be. What about her, Gallup? I suppose you've given the reciprocal side of matrimony some consideration."

"Yes," Gallup said. "I've thought as much about the ideal wife as I have about the ideal husband."

"Your opinion should be interesting, then. How would you define the ideal wife, Gallup? Can you give a definition?"

"Yes," the convalescent returned gravely. "I think it's simple. There are freaks and exceptions always, but in general it's pretty safe to deal with life on the principle that people will do unto you as you do unto them. An ideal wife is any woman who has an ideal husband."

The Doctor looked surprised; evidently he was expecting his friend's definition to be more elaborate. "What chance would either of them have to belong to your aristocracy, Gallup?" he asked. "They would be merely automatons mistakenly convinced that they were happy. If it is an automatic reaction for any person to do unto you as you do unto him and both of you are thus mechanistically moved by an insatiable urge to happiness——"

But at this moment the beaming Miss Cropsey opened the door, and, carrying her devoted patient's lunch upon a tray, approached him with obvious pleasure.

The Doctor decided that it would be tactful to postpone his argument to another day.

STARS IN THE DUST-HEAP

STARS IN THE DUST-HEAP

CONSIDER the Smith family of Topeka, Kansas. The Topeka Smiths were Twentieth Century people: they believed in education, prosperity and clean politics; and they knew a great deal about chemistry, mechanics, modern jurisprudence and music. There was only one point upon which they were curiously provincial, and that was geography. Mr. Smith, the father, had an inexplicable eccentricity: he was dismally superstitious about geography; and, marrying early, he was able to communicate this peculiarity to his wife so that she came to share it. Neither of them had ever been outside of Kansas, and neither wished ever to leave Kansas. If among their acquaintances there chanced to be one who, in their presence, referred to his travels, they looked vaguely distressed, and, as soon as possible, changed the subject. They brought up their children without any knowledge of geography, and taught them to avoid the mention of travel, as if such a topic were neither wholesome nor

polite, so that the children, too, got the habit of looking troubled and changing the subject whenever a
neighbour spoke of going away from Topeka. And
when any friend of the family did go upon a journey,
or, perchance, accept a business position in another
town, the Smiths would cease to speak of him, except when it was absolutely necessary, and they
would walk in silence if they passed the house he had
rented while he lived in Topeka. They made no
inquiries about him, and in every possible way they
tried to keep him out of their thoughts. They were
done with him if he left Topeka.

The insanest thing about all this was that the
Smiths knew that they themselves were going to
leave Topeka some day. Mr. Smith was the agent
for a harvesting machine; he had to go where the
company ordered him, and the company's policy
was to move its agents about at indefinite intervals.
Mrs. Smith and the children would, of course, have
to go wherever Mr. Smith did; yet they never allowed
themselves to think of anything outside of Topeka,
and they considered people queer and unreliable who
spoke unnecessarily of geography.

The harvester company sent Mr. Smith abroad.
The order came one day, without any previous

notification, and it was so imperative that he had no time to pack a trunk. In fact, he was at his office when he received the message, and he was obliged to leave without even going home to tell his family good-bye. Of course, finding him gone, they knew he had obeyed the company's order, and they understood that they must follow him; yet they made no effort to discover to what city abroad he had been ordered. They did not even make inquiries to see if there came a letter from him. He was no longer in Topeka; and that was enough for them. Everything beyond Topeka was the Great Unknown, and they shivered and sorrowed at the thought of it. Nevertheless, the whole family had to leave Topeka. The mother went, a year after the father; but the children did not try to learn where she had gone or if she had joined Mr. Smith. Then, one by one, the sons and daughters went; but those who remained in Topeka never tried to discover whither the others had betaken themselves or what were their experiences of travel, or the conditions in the foreign place to which they had gone. The Smith children still in Topeka knew all the time that they, too, would soon be going abroad, but they shiveringly declined to consider learning foreign languages, or even to look at time-tables and ask if anybody knew what to do for seasickness. Having the journey to make, they revolted at the mere idea of learning anything about what was at the other end of it, because in their hearts they believed that there wouldn't be anything at all at the other end of it. Sometimes one of them would murmur: "But if there should be——" And then he would shudder slightly, and close his mind to the idea, and return to his thoughts about Topeka.

To this day there are still some Smiths left in Topeka. They know they will not be there long, but they are making no preparations for travel, and they think that people who would like to know something about geography are rather crazy.

That is the "attitude of civilization" toward death and what may lie beyond death. Man, after a million years of the struggle to think, is still refusing to recognize as a fit subject for study that subject which most concerns him. Here he remains barbaric; he looks upon death as an ultimate horror that is "unwholesome to dwell upon." Man is still tribal in his attitude toward war because he is still tribal in his attitude toward death. Savages are somewhat more prejudiced in the matter. They will not mention the dead, fearing to be haunted, and consequently, though they sometimes have legends, the historian can trace fragments of their history only by digging up their burying grounds—an irony sufficiently grotesque. Man regards death as so horrible that when he reaches the utmost pitch of his rage he inflicts death upon his enemies. When he feels that life is unendurable he says the worst thing about it that he can think of: he says he prefers death. It is true that individuals, here and there, unbearably anguished by their lives, do long for death; and they think of death as peace, just as in the torrid days of summer we think of January as pleasant; and, seeking peace, they seek it blindly through suicide. But they do not know what they will find. In their utter ignorance, they guess; and usually their guess is that they will find nothing. Nevertheless, they may be like one of the Smiths of Topeka who decided finally that city life was not to be borne, and got on a train that landed him in Chicago. We do not know that death is nothing. If death is nothing, then we still know nothing about nothing. We know no more about death than prehistoric man knew. We know more than he did about how to postpone it, under certain conditions, and about how to alleviate the physical pain of it; and, using words interchangeably, we can make more definitions of it than he could; but our ignorance of death itself is precisely equal to his. This may be because we have preferred to cling through the ages to the superstition that we *could* know nothing about it.

There are minds that wrap themselves with satisfaction about a confusion of words, just as tangled thread loves to knot itself always the more inextricably. "Death is negation," they urge. "Death is merely not life. How can you state positives of a negative? You *can* know only nothing about nothing, so how can you know some thing about nothing?" But if they knew that death is nothing, and if they knew that death is not life, they would know more than Moses or Newton or Voltaire knew, and surely that would be knowing something. Enamoured of their wanderings with words, they do not even rise to the scientific height of a guess!

In man there is a profound, physical distaste for death which extends itself to become a distaste for the investigation of death: he lets his mystics and priests chant of it vaguely on ceremonial days; but he really does not wish to think about it at all. Therefore, he is naturally inclined to throw discredit upon investigations and investigators: in a sense, it is his instinct to do so. Moreover, certain thinkers (in their own distaste of the subject) have claimed that this very distaste is the only basis of man's hope of personal survival after death. They wish to dispose of the matter thus briefly, defining the theory of "immortality of the soul" as merely a by-product of man's instinct of self-preservation. And there are others who say that man got the notion that he had a soul through his savage ancestors' dreams: the savage woke from slumber and said, "I have been in strange places, obviously far away from my sleeping body. Therefore there must be two of me—the me of my body, and the me that leaves my body and goes away. Hence, when my body dies, the me that dreamed may still be alive." The civilized man's dream of survival is only a savage's dream after all, these rationalists say.

Thus they claim to have demolished the theory of survival. But, plainly, they may be (for all they know) exactly like the rational argufiers who may have said, in the year 1491 Anno Domini: "The earth is flat. Columbus believes it is round because his grandfather had a passion for round fruit, such as oranges and apples: the love of rotundity is inherent in his blood." To imagine the origin of a desire or a conception is not to prove that the thing desired or conceived has no existence, as any hungry child will demonstrate to the doubter's satisfaction.

The strangest theorist is he who takes the ground that man is actually indifferent to death (because, as death approaches, some men and most dogs appear to be indifferent to life), and that therefore, since death amounts to so little, it really amounts to nothing and coincides with nothingness.

There are a hundred other kinds of argufying, and most of the argufiers are Smiths of Topeka: they are superstitious about geography. Many of them are cocksure, and there is no other superstition so superstitious as cocksureness. And as the fundamental thing underneath the Smiths' superstition was their fear of a *possible* life (supposedly strange and uncomfortable) outside the walls of Topeka, so the fundamental thing underneath the superstition of many "skeptic" theorists is the dread of death as a queer and repellent life. Often they speak with a fierceness that betrays them: "Idiot!" they shout. "Don't you know it's been proved that you *can't* know anything, because there is nothing to know?" They love to make free with the word "proved"!

And with these argufiers march the literal-minded spiritualists, the great credulous crowd, gulled by their own imaginations. These are the people who dismiss investigation summarily when it reports evidence not in accord with their preconceived fancies of what "spirits" would do and say. They say they "don't believe in spirits," but obviously they do— even to the extent of having determined that spirits can never (for instance) be trivial or humorous; and with primitive naïveté they have so credulously pictured a heaven, or hell, of their own, that evidence of anything different seems to them nonsense. "Why don't the spirits ever tell us something worth while?" they say. "Why aren't the spirits more dignified? If they *could* communicate with living people, do you suppose they'd be talking about tin-types?" The spirits they believe in, you see, are already constructed out of fancies—imaginary spirits, finished in contour, gesture, and temperament—and anything purporting to be a spirit, but not fulfilling the ready-made portrait, is dismissed as either fraud or delusion. Thus the credulous immigrant might decline to take note of Ellis Island because no one met him with platters of money. "This is not America," he might say. "America is paved with gold."

And there are the other credulous: those who have a strange notion that Nature necessarily works with a kind of snobbishness or aristocracy of gesture. They look for the dramatic and graceful in her, expecting her to show forth something Grecian in great matters; they respect a thirty-knot battleship and forget Watt and his teakettle; they would like to see Ajax defying the lightning, but cannot believe that Ajax might better have understood what he was about if he had begun by rubbing a cat's back in the dark of a woodshed. "What!" they cry. "Look for the high dead among 'mediums,' 'psychics,' slate-writers, rappers, and trance babblers? Do you expect Moses to be rapping 'I'm all right' on a four-dollar table in a 'back-parlour' smelling of fried potatoes?" The seeker answers, "I do not expect Moses. I do not expect at all."

An inventor explained why the Wrights made an airplane that would fly. "They weren't graduates," he said. "They hadn't been conventionally educated in mechanics. They hadn't learned that certain things couldn't be done—so they did them!" This explains, incidentally, why genius usually comes from the country, and, pertinently, why it is scientific to keep an open mind.

Probably there is no mind that closes itself with gentler self-satisfaction than that which says, "We weren't *meant* to know." For thus we manufacture our own religion (frequently upon the spot and to suit the emergency of the minute) setting up a god in our own image and investing it with a wisdom wholly the fabric of our own inclinations and preferred ignorances.

"We aren't meant to know." . . . "We can't know." . . . "There isn't anything to know." . . . Those who prefer darkness may take their choice of the three "verdicts" still common in the Twentieth Century. But many people who say "We aren't meant to know," will deny their love of darkness. "We live by faith," they add. "We believe in the many mansions in His Father's house, and in 'If it were not so I would have told you.'" Yet they hold that there is a kind of impiety in seeking to follow this great hint of Christ's into further understanding of what He meant. *He* did not forbid: it is they who forbid. They say, "We are judged by the extent of our faith," which may easily mean that the harder a thing is to believe, the more credit to him who believes it. That is, the prophets did not do everything they possibly could to make their followers understand their meaning in so far as the followers' minds were capable, but, on the contrary, the prophets were deliberately puzzling in order to test the faith of the followers and make salvation difficult. Strange, for there are the parables to show what pains were taken to stir the least imaginative toward comprehending. Mystics always hope that science will some day overtake them.

The rich woman said to the socialist: "But it wouldn't be right for the world to have no poor. Charity is the greatest of all the virtues and there could be no charity if there were no poor." Her thought was not so far from that which maintains: "We were not meant to know, because knowing would leave no room for faith; hence efforts to know are irreligious." To live by faith is indeed not to walk in darkness; but it is to walk in only the dream of light.

But there are dreamers enough who think they have found true and actual light in their quest among the mountebanks and among self-deluded "psychics" and "mediums." Sleight-of-hand, cunning guess-work, and exhibitions of perfectly honest forms of catalepsy bring their rewards to both the performer and the bereft searchers for consolation.

It is not strange that eyes swimming in tears fill themselves with watery visions. That is what they want to do, poor things; and the frauds have only the task of suggesting how the stricken souls may deceive themselves.

The seeker for the truth about survival (whether the truth be consolation or not) must know that his way lies through a maze, which one enters trying to find a path that will take him out on the opposite side. There are a thousand fraudulent bypaths and he must learn to recognize at their entrances the little marks which show that the way out does not lie there—and yet the true path may be disguised by these same little marks. The seeker's heart must be steady and his head cool; he will see queer things at which he must remember to laugh, and his elbow will be plucked by hands reaching from many a curious cul-de-sac. If he becomes bewildered he will see things that do not exist, and he may begin to babble nonsense. And though he might never find the true path, he must not deny (if he would claim to have remained reasonable) that a true path may exist. In a maze, if there are a million paths, and a man, in his lifetime, explore nine hundred thousand of them, all leading nowhere, he is entitled to state

no more than his experience. His experience may
incline him to the opinion that no true path exists,
but all opinions have still the right to differ, so long
as they are but opinions. And if among the millions
of "spirit-messages" received through "mediums"
or "psychics," or what-not, by means of "slate-
writing," "automatic writing," "ouija-boards,"
"clairvoyance," "clairaudience," or any other generally uncredited and widely discredited manifestations
—if in all this vast mass of alleged evidence purporting through the ages to reveal the thoughts of "dis-
embodied spirits"—if in all this there be *one* veritable
message from a person whose body is dead, then the
case for survival is made: this dead person is alive
(or was alive after his death) and the possibility
of the survival of others is demonstrated.

And who could prove that there has never been
one such message? Only a person who had investigated and exposed *all* messages; and he could not
prove that a veritable message might not come in the
future.

We are dwelling in the night. To the man of ten
thousand years hence, who will not be able to distinguish, through his archæological researches, which
of the forgotten tribes fought the Great War that

left the long line of bones in the sub-soil from the Channel to the Alps—to that enlightened modern we shall seem to have been formless gropers in the dusk of ignorance. We do not really believe it, but that man of ten thousand years hence is actually going to live and speculate about us and study the dust heaps we shall leave. He will see that we were dwellers in the night—in the unknown. All this horror of death is horror of the unknown. Men face it magnificently. What would this mean: that they should face it knowing definitely what they face?

We make war, believing that death is annihilation. At least, we must believe that war means annihilation for our enemies. We (as tribesmen) may believe in a Valhalla for our own killed soldiers; but we must be convinced that our slain enemies are either annihilated or safely confined in hell. Otherwise, we are indeed mad. Surely it is insane for me to think I have settled all matters at issue between me and my enemy when I have shoved him out of a door through which I, too, must pass. Still, if we believe in Valhalla for our own slain, and in annihilation or hell for the slain of our foes, obviously we are on tricky ground, and probably General Bernhardi himself could not maintain such a point

and simultaneously maintain his countenance in
gravity.   No: war is made in the belief that death is
personal annihilation.

But if it isn't!

How if those thousands and tens of thousands and
hundreds of thousands of young Britons and French-
men and Hungarians and Italians and Russians and
Germans and Servians—and all those dead of
Belgium, and of our own, and all that mighty pro-
cession of the slain of Armenia—how if all these
hosts still live?

The expansionists, the imperialists, the pan-parties
who hope for "greatness" by conquest—these are
the fathers of militarism; that is, they are the fathers
of death.   Militarism is only another way of saying
wholesale-deathism.   And who can be madder than
a wholesale-deathist, since he knows nothing of what
death is?   The militarist, if he have any vestige of
even a cracked rationalism in him, must believe that
he betters his own condition by putting certain
people to death.   That is, he is like a doctor who, in
order to feel better himself, compounds an unknown
mixture from unlabeled vials and forces some one else
to swallow it; that is to say, he is a lunatic.   Inevitably he must be dealt with, and in our own

shadows we have no possible option: we can only fight lunatics with lunacy, heaping midnight upon midnight—wildly hoping in that way to use up such a quantity of darkness that light must take its place.

But lately was the whole world of one mind at last, bent upon one purpose, united in one thought; all mankind setting its giant energy to making war— that is to say, making death—without having first learned anything whatever of the nature of what it made! And those began this lunacy who most crazily *relished* it, and hoped most from it for them selves; if there be survival, what must be the condition of the spirits of such creatures as these? What sort of raging ghosts did they become?

But, if death were known, if it were no longer a mystery, but a condition familiarly understood, as the ocean is comprehended, for instance, by the untraveled midlander, then wouldn't the horror of war vanish and wars still be made? Probably the answer is that man will often consciously do horrible things but he will seldom knowingly do insane things.

The known is never horrible except as death or pain may come of it, and we begin to see that pain is only a prompting to us to educate ourselves in the law. "*Fear* is hell"—and we begin to guess that fear is only ignorance. All this horror of an inevitable condition—this fear of death, a fear which is an anguish even to little children—is wrong. The child fears the dark, yet there is nothing in the dark that is not in the light—except the light itself—and so there may be nothing in death that is not in life, if we had the light to see. If death is life, with "progress and problems," like those in what we call life, then we should not fear it. Or, if it were peace, we should not fear it. We fear it because we imagine it is darkness—yet that is one thing it *cannot* be. Nothing is not darkness. (For that matter, of course death cannot be nothing, in the literal sense. When we say "Death is annihilation" we mean only that "personal consciousness" does not survive the change called death.)

Pain is a hint for better education, and dread of death is a form of pain: it is a revulsion caused by the unfamiliar or the unknown. It is Nature kicking us for *not knowing*. In other words, horror of death, being in part our revolt against not knowing what death is—our fear of thinking about it—is what ought to make us think about it. So a child, locked in a dark room, will sometimes stretch forth his hand to explore, because his fear of what his hand may

touch is so great that he *must* explore. Fear should
be the ancestor of curiosity, and out of the hell of fear
may come that good thing, the wish-to-know. That
is the most benevolent of all the desires: in obedience
to it the boy takes a watch apart, to see what a watch
is made of; and a novelist takes life apart to see what
life is made of—for artists are only scientists working
in intuition instead of in a laboratory. But boys and
artists may only suggest things; they do not prove
them.

Now, certain men have said that they have evidence of survival, and some of these men are scientists
—even scientists by profession. If they have the
evidence they say they have, then it is going to be
possible to establish, before very long, the most important fact that can affect mankind. There is no
doubt that these men believe the evidence; and their
critics, unable to assail their sincerity, attack them
upon the point of gullibility. But this leads a person
of open mind to suspect the critics of a gullibility
of their own; that is, they may be gulled by their
prejudices. They are, indeed, thus gulled if they
declare Sir Oliver Lodge to be gullible because Sir
Oliver claims to receive messages from a dead person.
To show Sir Oliver gullible, the critics must prove the

messages to be fraud or delusion. They prove only
their own superstition who say, by implication:
"But spirits do not do thus-and-so; they do not speak
thus-and-so."

No doubt, serious investigators have been gulled:
that means nothing of importance; secret service men
have had lead quarters passed "on" them. The
question is, whether or not the investigators have
ever found true metal—if it were even a centime!
Most of them believe they have; and therein is a
circumstance of such significance as may give us
strangely to think, if we will take leisure to note it:
of all the men professionally of science who have
seriously and persistently investigated and studied
the alleged phenomena of "spiritualism," the overwhelming majority have drawn the conclusion, as a
result of their patient researches, that there *is* personal survival of death.

Only levity sneers at them now—at these patient
men who have sought truth in the dust-heap. They
have not yet failed; neither have they shown the
truth—if they have found it—so that all men may
see it and know that it is indeed truth. Their
task is heavy, but it is the greatest one, for it is the
task that must be done before civilization can begin.

To lift the burden of the unknown from the human soul—to destroy the great darkness: that is the work that engages them.   Man cannot be sane in the daylight until the night becomes knowable.

THE GOLDEN AGE

THE GOLDEN AGE

YOUNG people do not really believe that they are ever going to be old people. They often say, "When we get old," but they have no true conviction that they will ever actually "get that way." To the eye of youth, time is not really fleeting; time is long—so long that for practical uses the present appears to be permanent. Youth classifies people as old people, young people, and children; —to youth it seems that the old always have been old, and are to be everlastingly in that condition. And to a boy of twelve "old" means anything beyond the twenties; sixty hasn't much advantage over thirty-five, both appearing to be pretty dismal.

But during childhood and the earlier part of youth, there is a longing to be a little older, rather more prevalent among boys than girls. The little boy of eight looks forward to being ten, though interminable stretches of time seem to intervene. "Ten is a splendid age to be," the eight-year-old thinks yearningly.

"When I am ten, they'll let me ride a bicycle."
And at ten he wishes to be twelve; he will be permitted greater independence at twelve, and will be a
more competent and formidable person. Twelve
looks forward to fifteen. "At fifteen I can do practi-
cally what I want to. Grown people will listen to
me then, and pay some attention to my opinions and
my wishes." Fifteen wants to be twenty-one or
twenty-two. "I shall be a man then, and my own
man at that, independent of everyone except myself
and able to do whatever I wish. That is the Golden
Age."

At twenty-seven we have ceased to wish to be
older; for at that age we have begun to understand
why the figure of Father Time is represented with
wings, and we realize that our first youth is really
passing. At twenty-six there are hints of this
realization; but usually a man is twenty-seven or
twenty-eight when he begins to perceive that "there
is nothing permanent except change"; that he, too,
must change; and that some day he will, if he lives, be,
in actual fact, an old man. Girls begin to talk of
"getting old" a little earlier; but they mean "old"
marriageably, so to speak, and that they are too old
for the courtship of early-marrying boys. The

"oldness" of girls in the twenties has only to do
with young mating, and nothing to do with actual
age.

But for all young people, when the approach of
middle age is perceived to be a relentless and personal
fact, and there arrives that sense of a Golden Age in
flight toward the past, a severe melancholy often
attends the thought of such a change. There are
hours of brooding and of dismayed foreboding, for
we seem upon a down-hill path, with deeper and even
deeper glooms waiting for us below. Nevertheless,
at thirty, no one wishes to "go back" and live the
Golden Age over; and in our thirties, when we would
entreat our age to stand motionless, we impotently
find ourselves being railroaded toward forty, but no
wringing of hands will avail us; and so, all too soon,
we stand at forty—only to behold with horror that
fifty is already looming and imminent over us. And
yet—so strange and so contradictory are our lives—
at forty we would not "go back" and be thirty again.
Nor at fifty would we return to forty.

At fifty, however, we could more easily bear the
thought of returning to forty than to thirty; and at
forty the idea of returning to thirty is less uncomfortable than that of returning to twenty. In fact, at

fifty or forty we do not really look upon the twenties as having been a Golden Age for *ourselves*. We see youth disporting itself, slender, sound in body, and merry in the sun; and we say, "Ah, yes; that is their Golden Age!" But we know it was not our Golden Age. It was our most light-hearted age; but our light-heartedness, we know now, was only our child-hood still lingering in us. College commencements have their pathos for the middle-aged and elderly visitors, whose eyes grow misty as the graduating class files by; for age is touched by youth's un-consciousness of the things it has to face; and what moistens old eyes when they look upon youth is compassion.

It is true that age sometimes says, "Ah, to be young again!" But when age says this, it has in mind only the pleasures of some fugitive moment. The old gentleman upon the veranda might like muscles fit to vault the fence as his grandson does, or young heart enough to flit down a moonlit country road, as that grandson presently will, to meet a pretty girl at a garden gate; but he would no more change places permanently with his grandson than he would with his baby great-grandchild, screaming with the colic. When youth has moments of realizing the inevitable, youth dreads age; but not as age would dread youth, if youth came twice.

If we all lived to be eighty, and then began to grow younger, instead of dying, so that ten years after we had become eighty we should be seventy again, not only bodily but in experience, and if a decade after being seventy we should be sixty, and ten years later fifty, and thus drift down the ages of man to babyhood again, how would eighty view the approach of second youth and childhood?

Certain evanescent physical pleasures, so much keener in youth, might offer alleviations, but even they have their dark side, the colics of youth being keener, too. And who would be willing to surrender what experience has so painfully put into his head, and abandon whatever he has learned of wisdom in order to eat a bit of pie once more with the teeth and zest of eighteen? Who, indeed, would retrace backward the gathering of his wisdom through pain; for pain is the real teacher of wisdom. All in all, if youth were inevitable as the successor of age and middle age, any sensible man of eighty would look upon the approach of middle age with sharp discomfort; but from youth he would pray with all his might to be delivered.

"When we were boys," we sometimes talked of what kind of old men we should probably come to be. "I know what *I'll* be like," one boy said. "I'll be one of these funny-lookin' old men with little skinny legs and as big around the waist as if I'd swallowed a watermelon whole."

And upon that we all shouted with laughter, the prophet laughing more uproariously than any one else, because he had no idea, of course, that the figure he prophesied as his own future would bear any real relation to *himself*. He was a person of sixteen, and the caricature he pictured was of a queer old party probably more than thirty or thirty-five years of age. It didn't really matter what happened to any such swollen, old, thin-legged person.

So, too, when old men talk of what they were like when they were boys, they speak with impersonal amusement. "I was the worst idiot in town when I was eighteen," the chuckling old gentleman says, reminiscing with contemporaries. "I was idiotic *looking*, too; but I didn't know it, though I thought I knew absolutely everything in the world; and I took my own misinformed opinions for the law and the prophets. Of course I was heels over head in love with the prettiest girl in town; but that's as far as *she* went—she didn't have any more sense than I did, and I wonder now what on earth we talked about, because I used to talk to her by the hour. Then, one evening, when I was going to see her, it was pouring down rain in a February thaw, so my mother made me wear overshoes; and when I got to the girl's house I was in such a dreamy state about her I forgot to take 'em off and sat with 'em on, not knowing it. Her queer old father happened to come in and he looked at my feet and said, 'George, I'm glad to see you're so careful of your health that you don't mind whose rugs you muddy up!' It almost killed me! Mortified me so that I never went there again. Used to walk around that neighbourhood after dark, looking at the lighted windows, mooning about Polly and wishing I were a baker, with that old man dying of hunger and begging me for a crust of bread. Dear me, how often I've laughed over those days!"

When we are middle-aged or elderly, then our own youth seems to have been the experience of a generally absurd stranger. And in our youth we think of our own future elderliness as a grotesque condition with which we have no other than a merely humorous concern. Thus, in fact, every man, even to himself, appears to be not an individual but a little company of men, some of whom have not even a sympathetic understanding of one another. "The seven ages of man" separate him into seven different persons, any one of these having more or less acquaintance with the persons nearest him on his right and left, but no real intimacy with the others; while those at the extreme ends of the line are so different from each other that upon almost no subject whatever could their minds be brought to meet.

To know any man truly, then, and have his full portrait, we must look upon him not as an individual but as a company or group of individuals. No two of these people are in agreement on many points, and, although several of them may possibly hold the same general convictions, the tastes, pleasures, opinions, and habits of any one of them are in the main dissimilar from those of the others. There is little congeniality in this company, and only one of the members envies another; this is the Boy who would "change places" with the Young Man. The latter is the one of all the company most certain of his convictions, and among these is his conviction that he is the best of the lot—that his is the Golden Age. Is he mistaken about that, and, if he is, which one of the uncongenial company really possesses the treasure?

In my boyhood, I knew a man of ninety-five, a wise man and a good one all his life; but in his old age he had the habit of groaning. I don't mean that he was pessimistic; for he wasn't; nor was he a gloomy or depressing companion. He was clear-headed, entirely convinced of the upwardness of life and the universe; and he had no doubt that man is rising out of the beast and is going somewhere definitely, though not yet wise enough to comprehend the destination.

This old gentleman, who was born while the Terror reigned in Paris, who had been a soldier in our War of 1812, and was later an Abolitionist, had caught his own glimpse of the upwardness. He was discouraged, I supposed, about nothing under the sun—and yet he had that habit of groaning, of making long and emphatic melancholy vocal sounds. Sometimes, if you were in the room next to his, you could hear him even through a thick door. He would begin the sound at a high pitch and carry it down through a sort of vocal arc that lifted it again at the end. "*Oh, ho, ho, ho, ha, hum !*" There was impatience at the beginning and the end, and a weary patience in the middle; and I used to wonder what it meant; so one day I asked him.

I went in where he sat groaning beside his fire on a warm spring day, and I said, "What makes you do that, Grandfather?"

"Do what?"

"Groan like that?"

"'Groan'?" he said. "When did I groan?"

"Just now. For that matter, you do it dozens of times a day."

"No!" he said, and he seemed surprised. "Do I? I think you must be mistaken." Then he looked dreamily at his fire for a moment, seeming to forget both me and my question. "*Oh*, ho, ho, ho, ha, *hum !*" he said.

"There! You did it just then, Grandfather. Didn't you know it?"

"I believe I did groan then," he said. "Perhaps you're right. Yes, I suppose you must be."

"Don't you feel well?"

"Well? Yes, I'm not ill."

"Then why do you groan so often?"

"It must be," he answered thoughtfully, "it must be because I'm not dead."

That startled me. "Good gracious!" I cried.
"You don't want to *die*, do you?"

I might as well have been shocked by a starving
man's wanting food. My grandfather was a gentle-
mannered soul; but I think he may have been
tempted to call me an idiot. "*Don't* I, though!" he
said testily. "What do you imagine I want to stay
like *this*, for? Eyes almost useless, teeth gone, hearing bad, legs bad, back bent, fingers too warped and
shaky to serve me—and all of me useless to any one,
to myself most of all. 'Don't want to die!' What
on earth do you mean?"

So I understood that my grandfather had his one
discouragement: he was discouraged about dying.
He had been waiting so long that, although he still
had some remnant of patience left, he was getting to
be pessimistic about his prospects. He was living in
almost the last decade of years into which a man's
life can possibly be stretched; and his body had become altogether an annoyance to him. But even
had he been physically sound, I think he would have
wished to be "on his way," though not so impatiently,
perhaps. I did not understand his impatience then,
and it almost horrified me. Later, I perceived it to

be a natural feeling, not at all a morbid one and, in a way, enviable.

Men have shut themselves out of the world to attain to it; they have become pilgrims and monks and hermits, "mortifying the flesh," in order to obtain, with wisdom, that perception of the body as only a burden upon the spirit. And yet, although the age that brings a man so willingly to this threshold may well be thought to possess a lofty beauty, it is not the Golden Age of life, but a borderland age, like childhood.   For the first decade of our lives, the decade of babyhood and childhood, has its resemblances to the last one: the first is also a waiting; that is, a preparation, and has its own frequent reverie.   The child lives almost as much in his dreams of what will happen as the very aged man does in his dreams of what has happened.   The old man is adjusting himself to a new state of being that is almost upon him.   The child is adjusting himself to a new state of being that has just come upon him.   Moreover, there are sharper pains for the child in his period of adjustment to life than there are for the nonagenarian in his period of adjustment to death; and the child has less ability to bear pain.   We all, old and young, appear to be in the process of "getting put through the mill"; and childhood's wailings are eloquent of our early resistance to being shaped and standardized by the unyielding machinery of the mill.

That machinery is never quite done with us; we are never completed. All our lives, as in our birth and our death, we must do nothing except change; and change necessarily means adjustment; and adjustment means pain. Children come into life out of the nowhere, so far as we know, and everything in life is wholly new to them; necessarily, they have to get adjusted to everything.

The old convict "lifer," who had never been outside the penitentiary since he was sent in at twenty-two, came out at sixty-three, a free man. He stayed out three days and nights, but was back on the fourth morning, asking the warden to lock him up again. He could not adapt himself to the new world, and fled from it in terror, shirking the too great pain of the necessary adjustment. Children *can't* shirk it: no wonder they cry!

Some of them are born more philosophic than others; many of them have sunny dispositions; and all of them are capable of little ecstasies. Their happiness is unmitigated and flawless while it lasts; but so is their grief. We look at them as they play cherubically upon a green lawn at a "birthday party," and we say, "Oh, to be a child again!" meaning that we should like to feel again such pure and wholly unshadowed gaiety. But before the morrow most of the birthday party will have wept at least once; and when we see the tenement children at play in city streets and alleys we do not say, "Oh, to be a child again!" Childhood is not the Golden Age.

Nor is boyhood, which longs to be young manhood; but to young manhood itself the Golden Age usually seems to have arrived; and those living in it wish to detain it. "Rejoice not in thy strength," is advice pretty well wasted upon them. I have a neighbour of fifty-three who thus advised his son one day when I was present; and the son, a good-looking young man of twenty-six, laughed cheerfully.

"The trouble with you, Father," he said, "is that you're over fifty years old. You can't swim across the mouth of the river against the ebb tide, yourself, so you think it's dangerous for me. You don't realize the difference between twenty-six and fifty. You don't know anything about twenty-six."

His father took this a little irritably. "Don't I? I know what *I* was like at twenty-six. I thought nothing could happen to me."

"Well, nothing much has, has it, Father?"

"Hasn't it?" my neighbour returned. "You've just reminded me that I'm over fifty. *That's* happened, hasn't it?"

The son laughed again. "Well, do you regard it as a calamity?"

"No; but *you* would, if it happened to you, wouldn't you?"

"Yes, I think I should," the son admitted. "Yes, I'd hate like the dickens to be fifty; and when I think about it I don't see how you stand it."

"Don't you?" And at this it was the father's turn to laugh. He turned to me. "Hear that? The poor ninny thinks we'd change ages with him if we could!"

"Wouldn't you, honestly?" the son asked incredulously. "Do you mean to say sincerely that you'd really rather be fifty than twenty-six? On your honour, would you?"

He had become serious; but his father was amused. "That's characteristic of you, George. You can't imagine anybody's really wishing to be anything but what *you* are."

"I suppose it looks like conceit," said the son. "But I only mean it seems to me I'm better off than you are. For instance, take what we were just talking about. You think it's risky for me to swim the river when the tide's running out; but it isn't dangerous at all, and that's because I'm young and strong enough to do it safely. I'd hate to be fifty, because then I couldn't do it, and I'd be worrying, probably, about my son who could. Of course, that's not the only reason I'd hate to be fifty. One of the other reasons——" But here he hesitated.

"Go on with it," his father urged him. "You don't need to be tactful; we can stand it. What are your other reasons for hating the idea of being fifty?"

"Well, I'd hate having my life all arranged and settled and methodical, the way yours is. It seems to me the romance would be all out of things."

"I see." My neighbour nodded cheerfully. "You'd hate to be plodding along toward the grave—but still working to provide for your family—instead of going to a ball where you may meet a fairy princess and dance all night with her and perhaps run away with her in the morning. You wonder how I can stand it to know that such happy opportunities are not in my line any more. Also, you wonder how I can bear to *look* as I do."

"Oh, no, sir!" George protested. "You're still very—you still—you aren't——"

"I am, too," his father interrupted, relieving his son's embarrassment. "I'm fat—fat in the wrong places—and I'm rather jowled and rather wrinkled, and what hair I have left is going to be white before long. I can't trust my digestion; I don't *dare* eat a lot of things that you do, or at midnight as you sometimes do. I can't read without my glasses, and I often lose 'em. My doctor agrees with the government that I mustn't drink anything alcoholic at all. My dentist is threatening me with hand-made teeth. I can't play tennis any more, because my heart won't stand it. And, as you say, I can't swim the river— not even when the tide isn't running at all. Altogether, from your viewpoint, I'm in a pathetic condition. You wouldn't change places with me for a thousand mines of diamonds. Isn't that so?"

George laughed apologetically. "Well—I shouldn't like to change places with anybody."

"Listen to this, George," his father said. "I wouldn't, either. I wouldn't be in your place for a *million* diamond mines. Do you want to know why? I'll tell you; but I warn you that you won't understand it."

"Give me a try, sir."

"All right. Listen carefully, then," My neighbour looked earnestly at the young man, leaned toward him, and said solemnly, as if he were imparting something of the highest importance, "George, I don't *want* to swim the river!"

"Sir?"

"I told you that you wouldn't understand," his father said, relaxing his solemnity. "You feel sorry for me because I can't swim the river, and I feel sorry for you because you want to."

The young man sought to solve this puzzle. "You mean, then," he asked, frowning, "that as you got older you found you didn't care to do the things your age didn't let you do? Nature offers that consolation, does it?"

"You might put it another way, George. I stopped swimming the river while I was still able to do it. I didn't wait till I couldn't."

"Then why did you stop?"

"Because it bored me, George. I found that there wasn't anything in it, and also I grew wise enough to consider the danger. You tell me it isn't dangerous; but we both really know that what made me swim the river then, and what makes you swim it now, is the

very fact of the danger. It tickled my vanity to be
able to *beat* the danger. Well, in time I saw that
tickling my vanity was a stupid occupation. My
vanity got weaker and my experience got stronger,
I think. One reason I wouldn't change places with
you, George, is that I wouldn't go back to what we
call the 'vanities of youth.'"

"But I *don't* swim for my vanity's sake," George
protested. "I do it for exercise, and the pleasure of
being in the water. And as for saying that my liking
to feel strong enough to beat the pull of the tide is
'vanity'—why, that seems rather absurd, sir."

"Does it? You forget that I've done it, too, and
that I know now why I did it. It was for my vanity's
sake."

"It isn't with me," George insisted. "I know why
I do it as well as you know why you did it, don't I?"

"No, you don't; and now I'm going to tell you
another important thing, George, though probably
you won't realize its importance thoroughly until
you're fifty—maybe sixty. You *can't* understand
now why you swim the river, because you're still
swimming it. You're probably even too young to
know fully what I mean when I say that we can't
really know why we're doing almost anything *while*

we're doing it—especially in our youth. It takes
what's called a 'lifetime of experience' to enable a
man to know *why* he does things until long after
he's done them. Fifty is about as soon as that sort
of knowledge can be expected. I'll illustrate that, if
you like.

"When I was your age I was trying to persuade
your mother to marry me, and Charlie Simpson was
my rival. He's a good old soul, as you know yourself; but he was always 'a little wild,' as we say.
Well, I thought it was a sacrilege for a man like that
to come near your mother. I wanted to destroy him
for daring to dance with her. I looked upon him as
sheer pollution, and I remember telling her sternly
one night that I would offer no explanation, but that
my conscience made me bid her to take her choice;
if she had any more to do with Charlie Simpson, I'd
resign—so to speak.

"I felt I was doing the fine thing, the noble thing.
Either I would rescue that innocent young girl from
the approaches of the vile Charlie Simpson, or I
would quit, and go to China or somewhere, with the
remains of my horrified life. Bless your soul! I
like to have old Charlie around with us *now*—and
he's just as bad now as he ever was. I didn't dream

I was merely a jealous boy, Son; I thought I was St.
George! I'm offering that as a vivid and rough
sample of our not knowing why we do things *while*
we're doing them. But now that I'm fifty, if I got
jealous I shouldn't think I was noble; I'd know I
was just jealous. It's a priceless knowledge, my
boy, and we can't often get it at your age."

George laughed. "Are you sure of that, sir?"

"No," his father returned promptly. "I'm as
sure of that as I am of anything; but I'm not so sure
of anything, George, as you are of everything. That's
another reason I shudder when I dream that a mistaken fairy godmother—or some mischievous demon
—has made me twenty-six again. At twenty-six
we're so sure we know what's what that we go out,
sometimes, and actually get pretty well martyred for
a cause that ten years later we find ourselves oppos-
ing just as conscientiously and almost as violently.
Never mind!" He waved his hand as George showed
the impulse to interrupt him. "You're going to
ask me if the world doesn't need its martyrs, and
if it isn't necessary to believe in some things. Of
course, the answer is 'Yes.' But martyrdoms are
brought about by two cocksure parties in opposition,
you mustn't forget, each believing passionately that

it is right. There are martyrs who are mistaken, you know, Son; and it's a commonplace truth to say that it takes history to determine which were the mistaken ones. Well, at fifty-three, I've had twenty-seven years more of history than you've had at twenty-six. I'm at least that much nearer the truth when I'm no so sure I know it than you are when you're certain you do."

"Then, the way it seems to me," George said, "is that in at least some of my certainties I may be absolutely right, while in your uncertainties you're neither wrong nor right—so that really you can't be absolutely right about anything at all."

At this his father chuckled. "A fine bit of close reasoning, Son! The only trouble with it is that it doesn't allow for the human facts, and one of them is that upon great debatable questions in which the truth has the appearance of being upon both sides, uncertainty is the only wisdom. When time alone can solve a question we are foolish—which is the same thing in effect as *wrong*—if we insist upon championing our own solution. And when I said I wasn't so sure of anything, George, as you are of everything, I didn't mean I'm not so sure about a great many things as any human being has a right

to be. For instance, I'm that sure it was for my
vanity's sake I used to swim the river when the tide
was running out. At fifty we've got pretty close to
the truth about a number of things, because by that
time we have a sort of working-model of life, Son."

"I don't know what you mean, sir."

"No, you wouldn't. I mean that at fifty our lives
have taken a shape that to some extent we can see.
The fog has cleared away appreciably from the funda-
mentals, and the man of fifty knows that while he can
never wholly comprehend 'life, and the universe,'
he has at last obtained a fairly clear view—for practical purposes—of his own present relation to them.
He sees what they have done to him and knows
something of what they will do to him, and he has
learned that time does pass, and in its passage makes
many things right that seemed permanently wrong.
He knows, too, that he is presently going to be sixty
and then seventy—if he lives—and he knows he can
stand it all. His working-model of life, built up from
his thoughts about his experiences, is something for
him to 'go by' in emergencies and in trials. There's
less mist in his mind; he's reached a number of conclusions; he doesn't find himself beset by so many
problems. His working-model may not solve all prob-

lems; but it will rather promptly take them as near solution as they can be got."

The son did not appear to be satisfied. "Yes; but new problems are rising with each generation, sir."

"Or they may be old ones in new forms," his father suggested. "Of course, I don't claim that my own working-model may not be an old-fashioned one. Mine is founded on the *past* fifty years—I don't deny it may be antiquated—while the one you're developing for yourself is founded on the present day. Nevertheless, yours is fragmentary and incomplete and experimental. And, old-fashioned as mine may be, it has this merit: it works. That is, it does as far as I'm concerned. Looking back, George, I think that life was really pretty uncomfortable for me until I passed the birthday I had most dreaded, the fiftieth, and found that my working-model was complete enough to work."

"And yet, sir," George suggested, "I think you'd hate to be sixty or seventy almost as much as I'd hate to be fifty."

"No." My neighbour shook his head. "I don't dread those ages. My working-model shows me how not to dread anything. I've learned that fear is only a way of going through any tragedy more than once, or of creating a tragedy out of nothing. I've found, too, that there are mitigations to everything. Why in the world should I dread sixty and seventy or eighty, if I'm to last that long? Those are merely the calmer ages. The best things in life are at their disposal. All that you have, George, and that they have not, are the physical elasticities you use in doing things they don't *want* to do, and a few emotional intensities they thank heaven they are freed from. Another thing, my son, though you may be puzzled by it: so long as I don't try to do what you do and I don't want to do—so long as I don't try to swim the river—I don't *feel* a day older than you do. Not an hour! That's something I offer you for your encouragement when you shudder as you look ahead toward being older. It isn't a delusion and it isn't a senile boast; it's merely a fact. So long as we don't try to swim the river, we people of fifty and sixty and seventy—and even eighty, sometimes—don't *feel* old; not a bit more than you do at twenty-six. And with our working-models in good order we wouldn't change ages with you—not if we could swim all the way up the Mississippi and down again!"

George said nothing, but looked at his father skeptically, and the young man's thought was not

hard to read. What! Would his father not want
that brown hair back, and that slim and agile figure
and clear eye? Was not his elderly boasting only a
whistling in the graveyard, a mere bolstering up of
courage by making the best of what was miserably
inevitable?

But I, also, looked at my neighbour and con-
temporary, who was in fact a little younger than I,
and I knew that he serenely and entirely meant what
he said. For youth *need* not dread middle age or
elderliness or even old age. It will be "all right"
when it comes.

I remembered then that fine and true essay on age
written by Howells when he had passed eighty,
and wrote even better than he did at fifty and sixty
and seventy. He found all those ages agreeable, with
life more satisfactory than it had ever been before
fifty. Seventy to eighty he thought in some details
more satisfactory than any other decade; but walking
on level ground was a little too much up-hill if one
walked long. He found sixty to seventy to be the
competitor with fifty to sixty as the happiest age;
but, taking all possible advantages and disad-
vantages into consideration, he decided that fifty to
sixty is the Golden Age.

My neighbour and I, knowing that this was the award of a man over eighty and wiser than ourselves, are well content to accept his decision. Young George doesn't understand, of course. He can't bring himself to look forward to fifty with any pleasure. Nevertheless, when he reaches it he'll find that he, in turn, has come to the Golden Age. Not until then can he believe such a thing; but when he is actually living in it he will understand that he has wasted whatever time he spent in dreading it.

For the dread of being fifty is like many another of our fears. We behold an ogre upon the path before us; but when we reach him we see that he wears the kind and smiling countenance of a best friend.

HAPPINESS NOW

HAPPINESS NOW

TWO or three years ago, one of those little stories that go over the country came from a Boston clergyman of conspicuous veracity. On a New England country road he met an aged man who had been bedridden for several months, but was now up and about again. "I'm delighted to see you looking so well," the minister said. "I hope you've entirely recovered your health.'

"I'm getting along fine, thank you, Doctor."

"Have you a good appetite?"

"Appetite? I should say I have! Never eat so much in all my born days!"

"You sleep well?"

"Sleep?" the aged man exclaimed. "Never slept so good in my whole life! I'm in fine health, Doctor, fine!" Then he added cheerfully: " 'Course I've lost my *mind*, but I don't miss it."

Now I have heard kind-hearted people laugh at this little story—even kind-hearted people who knew the aged man himself and were aware of the calamity that had befallen him. Nor, hearing their laughter, did I find the laughers less kind-hearted than I had thought them, nor were they so. Nevertheless, there was something in their mirth that brought me to a question: How does it come about that gentle people can sometimes find calamity evocative not of their sympathetic pain but actually of their humour? And since tender-hearted people could not laugh at what they look upon as a calamity, the question may be put in another way: When do we feel that a calamity is *not* a calamity?

For the answer, I would go down to the village drug store opposite the post office. There the wise men collect before "mail time" every afternoon, and there, if you go often enough and listen long enough, you can hear anything. You will not need to go often, however, or listen long in order to hear something bearing upon the question about calamity.

"Yes, sir," one of the wise men tells the others; "George Thompson put every cent he had in the world into that mill, and now it's up and burned to the ground without a cent of insurance. Not a single cent! All George has got left between him and the poorhouse is that old nineteen-hundred-and-ten Ford he comes to town in, and his wife says he

still owes for *it*. Yes, sir; sixty-four years old, and
poor as the day he was born! They tell me his wife
is taking on something terrible. Neighbours say she
just sets in the house with her head in her hands—
kind of rocks back and forward, moaning-like—and
she hasn't had a mouthful of nourishment since the
fire, day-before-yesterday noon. They can't coax
her to. She thought she and George were all fixed
for their old age with that mill, and now it's gone, and
they're no better than beggars. She says she just
hopes to die. I certainly am sorry for that poor
woman!"

"Yes, and for poor old George too," a listener adds.
"It's a pretty dreadful thing to put all your eggs in
one basket, the way George did, and then drop the
basket. I certainly am sorry for George Thompson."

"For *George!*" the narrator of the misfortune
exclaims incredulously. "Sorry for George? Why,
to hear *George* talk you'd think he was going to have
that mill rebuilt and working away again inside of a
week! He's got no more sense of what's happened to
him than a rabbit, and you'd think he was pretty
near a millionaire right now, to listen to him. He's
talking just as big about all what he's going to do as

he ever did. It's the old lady *I'm* sorry for; but
George—my stars, man, don't waste no pity on
George !" The inference here seems to be that we
need not feel sorry for sufferers who do not suffer
(so to say) and we may draw the same conclusion
from the laughter of the kind-hearted people who
heard the story of the aged man's losing his mind
without being troubled by the loss. In each instance
calamity has befallen a person who seems unaware
of its gravity, and remains as cheerful after the misfortune as before. We may be astounded by such
cheerfulness; we may be amused by the incongruity
of it; we may be, indeed, contemptuous of it, or even
horrified by it; but so long as the victim retains it
we seem to feel that we may properly be at least as
cheerful as he is.

But this seems to imply another question: When
the victim of calamity realizes his misfortune, yet
retains his good spirits, do we feel that he has not
really suffered a loss at all? And again for the
answer I would walk down to the village drug store
and listen.

A troubled woman holding a sturdy little girl
tightly by the hand buys a "cough remedy" over the
counter. "It scared me so," she tells the druggist,

"I came right down to get something for little Rita."

"Has she been coughing very hard?" the druggist asks.

"No, not so very," the mother admits. "She only coughed a few times this morning, and it might of been a cough from the stomach at that, because she put too much molasses on her cakes for breakfast; but with anything like what's happened right next door, I expect I'm a little jumpy, and *any* kind of a cough from Rita scares me. Only nine days ago little Fanny Potter was playing with Rita in our back yard, and you wouldn't thought she could ever have a thing the matter with her. Nine days ago— and now she's gone! No wonder I don't like to hear Rita cough, don't you think so, Mr. Grewe?"

"Oh, I don't expect *her* cough's so very serious," the druggist returns. "How is Mrs. Potter taking her loss?"

"Oh, my!" Rita's mother moans. "I saw her for just a minute and I can't *bear* to think of her, yet I can't get her face out of my mind for a single minute. The minister's been there four or five times, working with her; but her family all say it hasn't done a bit of good, so far. If she could only be like Mrs. Will

Trueblood! When the Truebloods lost their little
boy, two years ago, of course Mrs. Trueblood said she
missed him terribly and all, but her faith upheld her.
She said she knew little Junior was a bright angel,
happy in heaven, and it would be impious to mourn
him overmuch. She could smile and not cry when
she spoke of him, almost right after the funeral, and
it wasn't painful at all to go there and talk with her
about it. In fact, she was so calm in her mind, it
was an inspiration and almost a pleasure, you might
say, to talk to her. If poor Mrs. Potter could only
take *her* loss that way, we'd all feel a great deal
better about it, Mr. Grewe."

Mr. Grewe agrees. "Yes, I wish she could.
She's a good woman and I hate to think of her in so
much trouble."

It is usually safe to draw general conclusions from
the conversations in our village drug store, because
most of the people who talk there are like most of the
other people anywhere in the country, and so, inter-
preting this little dialogue over the counter, we find
that if the faith of a bereft mother (or perhaps her
"philosophy") helps her to withstand her grief, we
can think of her almost cheerfully. And as what we
sympathetically lament, when friends of ours "lose

their money," is not the loss of the money, so, when
a mother is bereft, it is not the death of the child that
we most deeply deplore. What we "can't bear to
think of" is the unhappiness caused by the loss.

It appears, then, that for people in a state of bereavement, we suffer not in proportion to the extent
of the bereavement itself but in proportion to the
amount of pain we think it brings them; and that,
so far as our sympathies are concerned, we do seem
to feel that the victim of calamity has suffered no loss
at all if he has not lost his happiness. In other words,
if we accept the verdict of our feelings, there is no
loss except the loss of happiness, and so long as a man
retains his happiness he can lose nothing, no matter
what happens to him.

Now, thinking this over, I came to more questions:
But if a man loses his life? Don't we look upon that
as a loss of itself? Don't we feel that then he loses
anything except happiness? And again searching
light, I walked down once more to the village at
"mail time."

I reached the drug store just in time to save my
straw hat from ruin. A thunderstorm had been
threatening the countryside for an hour, and then,
after pretending to go away, it suddenly swung down

venomously upon our little town beside the river. It was one of those storms that appear to have personal intentions; it seemed to mean to wash the village into the river, meanwhile searching the place with lightning and cursing the inhabitants in the outrageous voice of immediate thunder. One of the wickedest discharges appeared to be meant for me in particular;—the floods descended, and with them a flash of intolerable light that seemed to explode upon my very eyes as I entered the drug store. "Murder!" I gasped, and leaned against the counter.

"What you makin' such a fuss about?" old Mr. Jezmiller asked brusquely. Mr. Jezmiller is one of our wise men, a former livery-stable owner, retired from business on account of automobiles, and crusty. "Nobody ain't murdered you *yet*, has they? So what call you got to be hollerin' 'murder' for, then, sence they ain't?"

"I meant the lightning," I explained. "It must have struck very close by."

"Didn't strike *you*, did it?" he said.

"No, it didn't, but I thought——"

Mr. Jezmiller interrupted me. "You 'thought,' did you? Well, the second you knowed you was thinkin' you knowed you wasn't ,struck, so what's

the use your makin' all this here fuss about it?   One
thing I never did have no patience with, it's people
that set up a squawkin' over a little thunder and
lightnin'. My soul! If you're struck, you're struck;
that's all there is *to* it. If you ain't, you ain't; and
so long as you ain't, what in the name o' conscience
are you *frettin'* about?"

I interposed an objection. "But that stroke was
so close I don't think I was quite sure it hadn't hit
me; that is, I wasn't sure soon enough to keep from
being nervous about it."

"Why, certainly you was," he said. "You knowed
you was scared, and long as you know anything at all
you know lightnin' ain't hit you, because if it hits
you, you don't know *nothin'*. That's the purest
kind of logic there is! When lightnin' hits you, it
don't give you no time to *worry* about it. Lightnin's
supposed to be kind of quick! Am I right?"

He appealed not to me but to a group of three or
four of our wise men who stood near by looking out
at the tumultuous water from the sky. They seemed
to feel that he was right, and he continued: "What
I always used to tell my first wife about a thunder
shower, I used to say, 'My goodness, ain't you got a
single *bit* o' gumption?' She was so 'fraid o' light-

nin' she'd always go put on her rubbers and stand with her feet in two glass fruit dishes in the middle of the sitting room as long as she could hear it thunder. 'My soul, woman!' I'd say to her. 'Lightnin's the one thing that don't give you time enough to worry about what's takin' you off. So why don't you behave like me, and get the good out of it by enjoyin' of yourself a-lookin' at it?' "

"That's so," Mr. Watson, the retired township assessor, agreed. "Yet I did have a second cousin get struck by lightning once I was right sorry for. He was a fine young man and left a wife and four little children. Yes, sir, I was right sorry for him."

Mr. Jezmiller seemed to feel himself challenged. "I bet you didn't," he said testily. "You *think* you did; but it wasn't him you was sorry for: it was his wife and children. He never had no time to suffer."

"I *was* sorry for him though," Mr. Watson insisted stubbornly. "I said I was, and I was. I was sorrier for him than I was for his family. He left them right well off, and after they got over missing him a little while they had no special cause to trouble. But he was a man just getting ready to enjoy his life first rate. He'd been nominated for

county treasurer that very spring, and he was sure
to get elected. He was looking forward to it, and
going to move to a nice house up at the county seat
and have a big time and all, and he was what you
might call kind of a happy-natured man, anyhow.
Do you mean to tell me, Mr. Jezmiller, that I don't
know what I'm talking about when I say I was sorry
for a man like that when he got struck by lightning?"

"No," his opponent admitted. "In view of his
likely goin' to enjoy makin' a lot of money out of the
county treasurership and all, it seems like a hard
case, and you got a right to claim you was sorry
he had to miss what he was lookin' forward to so
much. But what *I* say is: So far as just his gettin'
hit by lightnin' goes, you wasn't sorry about *that*,
or, if you was, you didn't show good sense. It's like
a boy, for instance, lookin' forward to show day.
Suppose his mother lets him oversleep that morning,
and he misses the circus parade. You don't feel
sorry for him because he was *asleep;* you only feel
sorry for him account of his missin' the parade. Well,
gettin' struck by lightnin' is prob'ly just about like
goin' to sleep right quick. You wasn't sorry for your
cousin because he done that; you was only sorry
about what he missed on *account* of it."

"I guess so," Mr. Watson said placably. "I presume you're right."

"You *know* I'm right!" Mr. Jezmiller corrected him. "Why ain't you man enough to say so?"

"All right," said the humbled Watson. "I know you are."

Now if Mr. Watson was well founded in this admission, and if Mr. Jezmiller was indeed right, then we look upon even the loss of life as of itself no loss to the loser. We say of a good citizen who has died that he was "a loss to the community," but it is then the community that we are sorry for; and sometimes we deplore the death of a useful man, saying, "He would have done so much good if he had lived"; but here again we lament for the survivors who lack his ministrations.

It is true that we may also feel sorry for such a man himself; but that is because we feel that doing good would have brought him happiness. A man may lose great opportunities, may lose his mind, may lose his liberty, his health, his life, his honour, or all of these and more; but if we think such loss entails no loss of his happiness, we feel no sympathetic suffering for him. The verdict of our drug store is

that for any individual there is no real loss whatever
except the loss of his happiness.

Long ago, in the village there was a boy who went
away to wrestle with the populous world. He became a power in the land, accomplished many things
for the good of his fellow men, and in time the village
was mildly proud of him. Yet at the drug store a
wise man said, one afternoon, "Of course he's a big
thing, and he's done plenty of big works; but I bet he
ain't a cent's worth happier than if he'd stayed right
here like the rest of us, and never gone away."

Another said reprovingly, "Ah, but there's things
worth more than happiness!"

"Are there?" the first said, with some satire.
"What are they?"

"How about success?"

"Success? What's a man go after success for,
except because he thinks it'll make him happy? It
don't always make him happy; but he wouldn't go
after it unless he thought it was going to."

"Well, then, how about the feeling that you've
done right? You know yourself a man'll often sacrifice his happiness rather than have the feeling that
he's done wrong."

"Yes, because he knows that though maybe he's going to feel pretty bad either way he'll feel *better* if he does right. He does right because he knows he'll get more happiness out of it than if he did wrong. That's pretty near the gist of the way all religions try to teach people how to live. They say, 'Do right and you'll be happier—not just now, maybe, but in the long run—than if you do wrong.' The way religions try to get people to *behave* is by working it into their minds that a certain line of conduct is the only thing that can make 'em happy; and they call that certain line of conduct the 'right' way to behave. That's because the old prophets of the religions were wise enough to see that no man ever did *anything*—not a single thing that he had any choice about—except because he believed that doing it was going to make him happier than if he did something else, or didn't do anything at all."

"Whoa up!" the other party to the debate exclaimed. "Hold your horses a minute! How about a man that gets into a fight, for instance? Suppose you say something to me that makes me mad, and I hit you. Well, you're bigger than I am, and I know mighty well that if I hit you you're going to hit me back—wallop me in the face, maybe, and make my nose bleed. Yet I'm so mad I don't take time to think, I just let out with my fist and land on you, even though I know I'm going to get licked on account of it. Do you claim I do that to get more happiness?"

"Certainly you do. You're so mad at me, just that minute, you can't stand the suffering of not doing something to me. You hit me because you think you'll get more happiness out of hitting me than you will unhappiness out of my hitting you back. No, sir; when you tell me there's things worth more than happiness, I say, 'Not to the human race, there ain't!'"

Then, as the other wise men nodded, agreeing with him, the verdict of the drug store appeared to be expanded. Not only is there no loss to the individual except the loss of his happiness, but the search for happiness is the motive of all free human action. Yet here there seems to be a contradiction, in spite of the fact that the wise men pride themselves upon their logic. If you are searching for a thing, then assuredly you haven't it, and if we are forever seeking happiness we are forever lacking it. And, lacking it, how can we lose it?

But the contradiction is not a real one; it is only

an apparent one. Of course, what the wise men mean is that we are forever seeking for more happiness than we already have; the happiness we already have is the one thing of value to us in our lives, our one possible loss; and that our great guiding desire is to keep it and add to it.

Our most important historical document calls it a self-evident truth that all men are entitled to the "pursuit of happiness." This does not mean that all men have no happiness, but that they possess a natural right to try to obtain more happiness than they already have. Evidently, then, to be occupied in the pursuit of *more* happiness is the normal condition of free men, and, thus, the Declaration of Independence confirms the verdict of the village drug store. To increase our happiness would then appear to be the natural business of our lives.

Now if this *is* our natural business—and when the drug store and the framers of the Declaration agree, the rest of us might as well take the matter as established—how shall we best set about that business? From one point of view we are already engaged in it, since all our deliberate actions spring from our desire to succeed in it; but any business (even a natural one) will "run" better, will have more chances for success, if it be carried on not blindly but with some understanding.

Considering this natural business of ours, then, we perceive that comparatively few people have *no* happiness; for a person who has none at all is a person who could be made no unhappier by any tragedy whatever. True, there are people who suffer grief so overwhelming that for a time they have no consciousness of happiness, and could feel no added misery if all mankind writhed in agony about them. But that condition is temporary, and the time of complete loss passes; for nature, having designed that man shall seek happiness, will help him begin to gather again something of what he has lost. Nature abhors a vacuum in happiness as well as in anything else.

So, in general, and at almost all times, we possess a certain amount of happiness—the "happiness we already have." I once heard this denied by a great authority: "Our happiness is only our unconsciousness of troubles that we really have." It was Mark Twain who spoke, and I had the greatest respect for everything he said, but found this whimsical, since it is quite as true (and more profitable) to say, "Our unhappiness is only our unconsciousness of blessings

that we really have." So long as we can lose any
happiness we possess some; and it is the truth that
most people possess more than they realize, for we
know how pathetically often loss reveals what a great
quantity has been possessed but not realized.

We all of us count over our worldly goods now and
then.   Even a child will do that, making a sort of in-
ventory of his toys, and, as we grow older and more
accumulative, we continue the habit; but we do not
often take stock of our happiness itself, and when we
do we are likely to do it pessimistically, and without
a proper sense of proportion.   This is in great part
because of our strange disposition to concentrate our
attention upon even a temporary annoyance, thus
giving it disproportionate importance and making it
acute—and there are few times in our lives when we
are not beset by at least one annoyance.

It is mainly by our habit of putting inevitable but
relatively unimportant annoyances in the forefront of
our lives that we mar and obscure the happiness we
already possess—what Dr. Samuel Johnson called
our "comparative happiness"; and in this we are
like a painter who might paint pretty good pictures,
but in every one of them gets a small blemish into the
foreground, where it becomes so **conspicuous that**

the whole painting is valueless.   If a painter did such
a thing deliberately, we should not think him rational;
yet it is what many of us do with our own paintings.
We do it though we know we do it and have been
preached at about it a thousand times.

Our mistake is in stubbornly forgetting that we
have a choice in the matter; in stubbornly forgetting
that we need not keep in the background the happiness we already have.   With absurd but determined
obstinacy we imprison it behind our annoyances and
our worries—worries, usually, that spring from fear;
and in regard to these fear-worries of ours, almost
any habitually worrying person may astonish himself by a little mathematics.   If such a person will
take notes of his worries for a year, or perhaps for no
more than a month, setting them all down on paper
faithfully, and if he will then review them arithmeti-
cally, he may discover something surprising about
happiness, and also possibly about himself.

In his review he should place in one column all his
worries that have proved to be unwarranted, or
founded entirely upon pessimistic imaginings; in the
other he should set down the worries that have had
good cause, the anxieties justified by disastrous facts.
A worrying mother who once did this found at the

end of a month that she had items in only one
column; and she declined to proceed further with
her notes. She said it was an idiotic thing to be
doing, and anyhow she *might* have been right about
any or all of the worries that had merely happened
to be unfounded. Likewise, a fretful business man
who made similar lists, and at the end of nine weeks
found that his justified worries came to nineteen
and his unjustified ones to four hundred and thirty-
seven, refused to continue the system: he said it
was "too mortifying."

But although neither of these people gave mathematics a fair trial, as a cure for obscuring their
"comparative happiness" behind mere gloomy
imaginings, both of them were observed to be of a
cheerfuller and more sanguine outlook on life ever
afterward. "Actual statistics" have their uses
sometimes.

One afternoon not long ago, I heard two old men
talking of what they would do if they could "go
back" and live over their active lives with the advantage of the wisdom that experience and age had
given them. One of them said, "If I could be young
again and live my life with what I know now in my
head, I wouldn't bother so much about trying to get

down to the office before anybody else, the way I
used to. I never took a holiday till I was past forty-
five. All I knew or thought about was my business.
If I had it to do over, I'd take more leisure; I'd take
time to look around me and enjoy myself as I went
along."

"Yes," the second said. "But that's just what I
did, and it hasn't turned out very well. I thought
there'd be plenty of time for business by-and-by;
I frittered the best of my youth and younger middle
years away just looking about and having a fairly
good time, and that's the reason I'm spending my
old age in harness, still having to try to earn a living.
I wish I'd worried a little more about that in the
days when I was young and husky!"

"You do, do you?" the other inquired. "Well,
that's just what I wouldn't do."

"You wouldn't try to put by something for your
old age?" his friend asked, surprised. "You wouldn't
be industrious in your youth so that now——"

"I didn't say that," the other interrupted. "I
didn't say I wouldn't do it; I said I wouldn't worry
about it. I've been looking back over my life pretty
thoroughly, as we're likely to do in these days when
our legs and eyes fail us and, unless somebody talks

to us, or reads to us, or takes us for a drive maybe, we can only drowse or rummage up old pictures out of our memories. Well, I see that I was an idiot to be a worrying man."

"You think so? But that's just what made you succeed. It's what built up the fortune you're enjoying now."

"No, my worrying didn't do that; my energy did it—my energy and my carefulness—and, as I say, I made a mistake to devote all my attention to business. But my much greater mistake was in worrying. If I had my life to live over, I wouldn't worry about anything at all."

"But that's impossible," his friend said. "There were times when your business seemed to be going the wrong way, and if you hadn't worried you wouldn't have worked so hard to save it."

"Yes, I should, because I worked just as hard when things were going well as when they weren't. I worked my hardest all the time. I'd have saved my business more easily when I seemed to be near losing it once or twice, if my calmness and cool judgment hadn't been disturbed by the worrying I did. Worrying isn't what gets most things done, though I'm willing to admit it often gets a lot of useless

things done. My worrying over my business only
made the business harder for me. If I'd had sense
enough to leave out the worry, I could have made
the business itself a pleasure, and of course that's
what every man's business ought to be. No, sir;
I tell you that if I had my life to live over I'd never
worry about anything in the world."

"But there's more than business to worry us,"
the other reminded him. "There's danger and accident and sickness and death."

"I know, and I don't forget those things. When
I say I wouldn't worry, I don't mean I should be
spared from all sorrows. I mean that I wouldn't
anticipate them; I wouldn't trouble myself by fearing them before they arrived—that is, when they
didn't exist—and I wouldn't create unreal ones in
my imagination. No; I've been looking back and
counting up the sleep I lost and, what's worse, the
peace of mind I lost, in the pure folly of worrying,
and I've been able to calculate that ninety-nine
hundredths of my troubles were fears of trouble.
Yet I'd let these *phantom* troubles bother me as
much as the one percent of worry that was founded
on fact. What's more, I couldn't distinguish between the worry that was founded on fact and the

worry that was pure phantom, and since my worrying founded on fact didn't of itself improve the fact
any, what a loss I had through the whole mass of my
worries! If it hadn't been for them, I'd have had
the blessed understanding that I was living about as
happy a life as a man *can* live. Just think of it! If
ninety-nine percent of the worries of most of us are
made out of nothing (and they are) and if we can't
tell the difference between any of them and the
one percent that *is* made out of something, and even
with that one percent the *worry* doesn't help the
something, isn't it pretty stupid of us to worry about
anything? I don't mean that if I had my life to live
over I shouldn't take every possible precaution
against accident, or that I shouldn't send for the
doctor when I got sick; but I see now that all I accomplished by worrying was to waste the greater part
of my happiness, and I tell you I shouldn't be such
an idiot as to do it again."

"But our real troubles———"

"I'm talking of worrying!" the old gentleman insisted, a little sharply. "I said I shouldn't expect to
be spared from sorrow; but I'd at least have sense
enough to smell smoke before I'd think the house
might be on fire, and I shouldn't trust to just smell-

ing it, either.   I'd have to see it, and where it came
from."

"But suppose the house burned down.   Wouldn't
you worry then?"

"Worry after the thing was *gone ?*" the old man
cried.   "That would be a fine way to take time out
of planning a fireproof house!   And yet it's one of
the very ways I used to waste my time, and the funny
thing is I *knew* I was wasting it.   That's the queerest
of all."

"What is?"

"That I knew what I was doing," said the old
gentleman.   "I knew all the time I wasn't accom-
plishing anything by worrying.   I knew I was doing
no good, but only torturing myself by it.   Then
what, in the name of common sense, did I do it for?"

Listening, I thought that this was a wise old man,
but that his wisdom came too late in life for him to
take much advantage of it, because, unhappily, he
couldn't live his live over in the manner he and his
friend were discussing, nor, indeed, in any manner.
What seemed most regrettable, here he was, at
eighty-five, realizing that all along he had possessed
the power of choice: he could have enjoyed all the
peace of mind, all the happiness he had spoiled, if

he had realized at the outset that he possessed that power.

So then, thinking of the happiness we already have and how to preserve it, I came to the conclusion that we must first realize that we have it, and then take stock of it, so to speak; and that to preserve it we must perceive our power of choosing whether or not we will mar it with our uneasy imaginings. For, if we do but see that we can choose whether or not to mar it, of course the choice is made. The difficulty is only in perceiving that we have the choice.

Then, if the natural business of man is not merely to preserve his "comparative happiness" but to add to it, how shall he set about the addition? Here is a ticklish question, for if we fail in our business of getting more happiness than we already have, we inevitably lose some or most of what we have. Therefore, should we not best be content with what we have, and make no effort to get more? But we *cannot* be content with the happiness we have: a man can be content not to increase his goods or his money; he can know moments, too, when his happiness seems complete and ineffable; but they are only moments of temporary delusion. No; the business nature has ruled for us is getting more happiness than we already possess, and here we have no choice, for nature has permitted none; we *must* all be about that business. The question is how to be about it.

Disappointment, little or great, is a part of almost our daily life, but is not always the result of our failure to get what we thought would make us happier. We are constantly deceived about that; we do a thousand things, thinking they will make us happier, and they don't. We set our hearts on reaching certain heights above us; it may be on certain ambitions, thinking that when we attain them we shall be happier; but when we do attain them, we may find our happiness not increased but lessened. We cannot trust our desires, our ambitions, or even what we think are our needs—not even our consciences—to make us happier. Where, then, is a surer guidance?

And again I fall back upon the wisdom of the drug store.

"I never in all my life knew any such a couple as Henry Strout and his wife," said old Mr. Tomlinson, the retired hardware dealer, edifying us there, the other day. "In the way they disappoint themselves, I mean," he went on. "I never knew a couple in my life to be so enthusiastic about what they were *going* to do, and then be as low-spirited after they got it done. When they were courting each other, Henry seemed to think he was going to own the United States if he could get Ellen to say 'Yes,' and after they got engaged Ellen told everybody she'd be the happiest woman in the world as soon as she was married to Henry. Then, when they'd been married a little while, she said if she could just cure Henry of smoking, she'd be a happy woman; and she did cure him, and they both had a mean time of it and talked to the neighbours about each other a good deal. After that, they bought a lot and began building a new house for themselves, and you'd of thought it was going to be the Capitol at Washington. Both of 'em said, just wait till they got that house finished, they'd be the happiest people in the world. But after they'd moved in they were awful blue. The plumbing and everything else was wrong, according to the way they talked; and they'd built it just the way they wanted it, too. I never did know such a fool young couple!"

"What's wrong with 'em now?" Mr. Watson inquired.

"It's the baby," Mr. Tomlinson said. "They told everybody, just wait till they began to raise a

family, then they *would* be happy!   Well, at last they
got their way and the baby's here.   Henry's all
upset over it because it's only a girl, and Ellen cried
because it's a blue-eyed blonde and she wanted a
brunette.   They get everything they set their minds
to, and it always makes 'em miserable."

Mr. Watson shook his head.   "That's because
they don't set their minds the right way," he said;
and as Mr. Tomlinson made some sounds indicating
mystification, he amplified the statement, "Henry
Strout and his wife keep disappointing themselves
because they think *they* know what's going to make
them happy.   Well, they don't know, and that's
easy to prove, because first they thought it would be
getting engaged, and it wasn't.   Then they thought
it would be getting married, and it wasn't.   Then
they thought it would be having a new house, and it
wasn't.   Then they thought it would be having a
baby, and it wasn't.   Well, they think the house
and the baby didn't turn out just the way they
expected, and that's why they're so blue; but it ain't
so.   They'd have got less happiness than they expected out of the baby and the house no matter what,
just the way they did out of getting engaged and
getting married.   They'll be miserable off and on

all their lives, unless they get over thinking *they*
know what'll make them happy."

Mr. Tomlinson evinced further mystification.
"What on earth are you talking about?" he said.
"What else have they got to go by?"

"Plenty," Mr. Watson returned serenely. "Did
you ever know anybody that could trust his own un-
aided judgment about what'd make him happy?
No, sir! If I went blundering around, doing just
what I feel is going to make me happy, I'd land in the
poorhouse, like as not, or in the insane asylum, or
maybe in jail. It's a thing you got to use your
common sense about. There's natural laws about
what'll make people happy, just as there's natural
laws about everything else."

"I suppose you think it ought to be taught in
school," Mr. Tomlinson suggested, in the tone of
satire.

"Why not?" Mr. Watson promptly returned.
"They try to do a little of that kind of teaching in
Sunday-school, anyhow. Don't they tell the children 'Be good and you will be happy'? Well, it's
true, too, I expect; but the trouble is it's so hard to
see just what is being the *kind* of good that makes
you happy. A person can usually obey the Ten

Commandments without much trouble; but most of
the time just merely not breaking one of 'em doesn't
make him any happier.   What I mean is that if I
want to be happy, I better use some *system* about it.
We study the best ways to get everything else; we
study the best ways to get knowledge; we study the
best ways to get health; we study the best ways to
get prosperity; we study the best ways to get good in
our morals; but we don't study the best ways to get
happiness."

"No?" Mr. Tomlinson inquired, again satirical.
"If a man had acquired education and health and
prosperity and good morals, wouldn't he be pretty
happy?"

"Certainly not," Mr. Watson said stoutly.   "He
could have those things and a great deal more, and
just as like as not he wouldn't be any *happier* than
some darky with a watermelon, or one of these section
hands working on the railroad and getting enough
money to go back to Italy and buy a farm.   You
know that yourself, Tomlinson."

Mr. Tomlinson looked cross.   "I waive the point,"
he said impatiently.   "What are you trying to bring
out?"

"Why, just this.   When we want to get strong,

for instance, we look around and see what makes other people strong as a general *rule*. We notice that some of 'em have been *born* strong; but that's not going to help *us;* we've got to pattern by the people that have got strong through a certain line of conduct. So we see that they eat strengthening foods and take strengthening exercise regularly, and don't do things that weaken 'em; and we can go and do likewise, and get strong too, or anyhow stronger than we were. We don't act any way like that to get happier than we are; but we *could*. We could study the happiest people we know of, and find out what makes 'em that way."

"Well, what does?" Mr. Tomlinson asked challengingly. "What does?"

"A good many things," Mr. Watson answered and, as Mr. Tomlinson laughed contemptuously, added in haste, "*I* know that's a pretty general statement; but I mean special things."

"Name 'em," said Mr. Tomlinson. "Name 'em."

"I was going to: Faith, for one thing. You take people that really believe in their religion. Can you deny it makes 'em happier?"

"No, I don't," Mr. Tomlinson replied shortly. "Name some others."

"Being busy," Mr. Watson said. "Being busy at something interesting. If a man isn't interested in the work he's *got* to do, he'd be happier if he found something to do that would interest him outside his other work. Wouldn't he?"

"Suppose he couldn't," said Mr. Tomlinson. "Suppose the work he didn't like took all his time."

"Then he'd be happier if he did it his very best, no matter how much he didn't like it, because people are happier that do their best, no matter what they do, than people that don't. I don't claim it makes 'em absolutely happy—that's not what we're talking about. Nobody can get strong enough to lift an elephant, no matter how strong he gets; but an ordinary man that isn't strong can always get stronger than he *is*."

"All right," Mr. Tomlinson admitted. "Go on with your namin'."

"Well," said Mr. Watson, "I believe it would be a good thing to look over all the people you know, and decide which of 'em have the happiest expressions on their faces. That ought to be a good way to tell. Now, when I do that—when I think over the usual expressions of all the people I ever knew—I believe the very happiest expressions belong most to one kind of people."

"What kind?"

"Not you or me," Mr. Watson said gravely. "I mean the kind of people that make other people happy. You think over all the people you've known in your life, and see if the happiest expressions didn't belong to the people that made other people happy."

Mr. Tomlinson contained his indignation with difficulty. "My! But you're telling us something new!"

"I'm not trying to tell you anything new," Mr. Watson said. "I'm trying to tell you something that's *so !*"

"It ain't so about you and me," Mr. Tomlinson said sharply. "*I* can't learn how to get happier that way! The people that make other people happy are born unselfish, and mighty few of us are born that way."

"Well, mighty few of us are born real strong, either," said Mr. Watson. "That's no reason we don't try to get stronger. If we see that people *are* happy who make other people happy, why don't we practise it a little ourselves?'

"Go on!" Mr. Tomlinson said unkindly. "That's

been preached at us for a thousand years, and never
has done any good yet!"

"Then if it never did, it shows up our dumb-
headed stubbornness pretty strong! We want to
be happier than we are and for a thousand years
we've known *how*—and yet we won't *do* it!"

"We deserve what we *get*," Mr. Tomlinson said
with emphasis. "I don't see as you've increased
my knowledge much of how to get any happier. I
knew all you said beforehand."

"Yes, but you won't act on it—because you still
think *you* know how to be happy better than nature
can show you! The way's open, and yet, after a
thousand years, people like you won't take it!
When you get over your stubbornness you'll enjoy
life better, Tomlinson."

At that Mr. Tomlinson's expression became em-
bittered. "'Enjoy life'? Nobody enjoys life!"

"They do, too."

"Who does?"

"Well, you've admitted yourself that certain kinds
of people do—the ones that make other people
happy, for instance. And there's another class that
enjoys it most of all maybe."

"What class?"

"Well, sir," Mr. Watson replied, "I'm thinking now of the class Henry Strout and his wife would belong to if they'd let themselves. I mean the young couples that are raising little families—though I don't put any age limit on this class exactly, and almost anybody that's got something ahead of him he's working for could belong to it. But in general it would include the fathers and mothers that are trying to get on in the world, and using their energy and carefulness to do it, moving ahead, little by little. Sometimes they slip back some, maybe; but they've learned that if they keep on working and trying they *will* get ahead *some*time. Those are the people I think are maybe the happiest, Tomlinson."

Mr. Tomlinson uttered a chilling sound of laughter. "They are? Why, you've picked out the most anxious class of human beings we got in our whole country. Don't tell me I don't understand what class you mean, because I do. You mean just the average run of folks, fathers and mothers mostly, that haven't got as well off yet as they mean to be, and are trying to be—with the father working his hardest in an office, or a store, or a factory, or at a trade, or on a farm, maybe, and the mother looking after the children and trying to do her share. Why,

you talk about judging people's happiness by their
expressions; those are the very people that look the
worriedest! You know who they remind me of?
If you can tell anything by expressions—the way
you say, Watson—why, these people you claim are
the happiest remind me of the folks in an automobile
that is going pretty fast—the folks that aren't running it. All they think about is getting where
they're going to; but they aren't sure they'll get
*any*where—except in the ditch! And you call
them the happiest!"

"I do," Mr. Watson insisted desperately. "And
if they aren't, the only reason is that they don't
know how happy they really are!"

There was a shout of laughter. The wise men
standing near by considered him defeated and his
final assertion preposterous; but as I walked home
I began to think about Mr. Tomlinson's comparison
of Mr. Watson's happiest people to anxious people
in a motor car, and I wondered if both Mr. Tomlinson and Mr. Watson mightn't be right—Mr. Watson
particularly.

I had lately been upon a long motor journey myself, in foreign and interesting parts of the world; and
one day, when it was more than half over, I dis-

covered that I wasn't enjoying it nearly so much as I could. I found that I was thinking almost continually of the speed we were making and of the earliest possible hour of arrival at the town that was our evening's destination.

There was nothing I wanted to do or see in that town—it wasn't nearly so interesting as the Arab countryside we were traversing—yet my attention was concentrated on getting there. This, I discovered, had been my frame of mind day after day on all the long journey; and yet, at the end of each day, as I went to sleep in the hotel, what my mind dwelt upon with most satisfaction were the roadside pictures I'd been seeing throughout the run. Moreover, I had gone abroad for the motor journey itself, not for its daily destinations—and here I was occupying my mind and worrying it with those unimportant way stations.

I reformed myself successfully. When we were on the road, I said to myself, "You came across the seas to be doing what you're doing *now*—not to be getting to various sleeping places. You came for the *Road*."

I think my facial expression thereupon underwent an alteration that might have pleased Mr. Watson.

My anxious look departed—undoubtedly I was happier.

And so, walking home from the village drug store, I concluded that Mr. Watson was, of them all, nearest right, when he made his desperate final statement after Mr. Tomlinson's overwhelming argument. Those happy people Mr. Watson meant to describe —the "average run of folks, fathers and mothers, mostly, that haven't got as well off yet as they mean to be," have forgotten the joy of the Road, when they "don't know how happy they really are."

We add most to our happiness by knowing that we are happy. Some day Mr. Watson's happy people —who are at the same time Mr. Tomlinson's most anxious people—will say, "Ah, we were happy *then!* Those days of the struggle upward, full of anxieties and disappointments and gains and setbacks, *they* were the happy days. Queer, we didn't realize it then and enjoy it more!"

For it isn't the destination that makes us happier. "We came for the ride"—not for the end of it.

THE END